South of Heaven

Erin Louis

Dedication

For my mom Kathryn, not Kathy, who may or may not be in Heaven, but was my guardian angel on earth.

South of Heaven

Prologue

Her legs dangle off the edge of the pew, and she tries to remember not to swing them. She is trying to pay attention to the priest, but the more she tries to focus on his words, the more her legs want to swing. Kat doesn't think she can listen without swinging her legs. She's aware of her mom next to her. She is not looking at her, but Kat knows she's just waiting to elbow her if she thinks she's not paying attention or if she is caught swinging her legs. It is a formidable quandary for a six-year-old.

She decides she should try to listen, as her mom may ask her about it later. She won't get to watch the "It's the Great Pumpkin, Charlie Brown" later tonight if she answers the wrong way, revealing that she was not in fact paying attention. Halloween is her favorite holiday. She got in trouble last year and she wasn't allowed to watch it. Her best friend Christy was allowed to watch it though, and Kat was still pretty mad about it.

She hones in on what guy in the funny clothes is saying

at the front of the church.

"For 'God's only begotten Son… has won a treasure for the militant Church… He has entrusted it to blessed Peter, the key-bearer of Heaven, and to His successors who are Christ's vicars on earth, SO THAT THEY MAY DISTRIBUTE IT TO THE FAITHFUL FOR THEIR SALVATION."

Why is he yelling? Her eyes drift to the large cross with the dead guy on it behind him, and she cringes. *Yuck.* And then immediately regrets the thought. *Sorry Jesus, you're very handsome.* Her mother told her that God hears every word she thinks. But bad thoughts are ok as long as you say you're sorry. Kat apologizes for bad thoughts all the time. Sometimes for bad things too, like when she knocked Angela's milk off the table for calling her a poopyhead. Kat still thought she deserved it, but she apologized anyway. Jesus died for our sins, but only if you apologize for them. Kat wanted to make sure she went to Heaven because Hell didn't seem like all that much fun.

"All children of the Church should nevertheless remember that their exalted condition results, not from their own merits, but from the grace of Christ. If they fail to respond in thought, word and deed to that grace, not only shall they not be saved, but they shall be the more severely judged," the priest said, lowering his tone, to Kat's relief. *More severely judged, that means Hell*, she shuddered.

She receives a jab from her mom's elbow into the meaty part of her upper arm, and she realizes she's been swinging her legs again. It didn't hurt, but she's scared she may have blown her chance to watch Charlie Brown. Again. She pictures Christy's smug face and redoubles her efforts to behave.

Her mom stands up and walks to the edge of the pew.

Kat has to stay there, but at least she can swing her legs for a while as her mom and the others get their blood and flesh. *Ew, gross. Oops, sorry.* At this rate, she's not going to make it to Heaven. She wonders if the wine and cracker tastes like blood and flesh. She will get communion next year, and she's dreading it. Her mom told her it is only symbolic and that it transforms into the blood and flesh of Jesus after you eat it. Kat wasn't so sure. She was, however, kind of excited about the new dress for the occasion.

Getting to Heaven seemed awfully complicated. She figured most of it she just didn't understand, being a kid and all. But she is afraid of Hell. She saw the devil in cartoons poke people in the butts with his fork, but she thought the actual Hell was probably much worse.

Chapter 1

She lifts her hips up to meet his, and tilts her head back, lost in exquisite ecstasy. Kat thinks his name is Chris, but isn't sure, and in the grips of an intense orgasm, doesn't care. He goes deeper for a moment, intensifying her pleasure, before rolling off her with a long-satisfied sigh. Kat lays there for a moment, letting her body relax and her breathing return to normal. Chris, or whatever, ruins the whole thing by speaking.

"Wow, that was great," he said, still breathy.

Kat plots her escape. If this guy gets all attached, she'll have to find another bar.

Kat sits up in *I'm pretty sure it was Chris*'s bed, not bothering to draw the sheets up around her naked body. He looks at her lovingly, and she turns her head so he can't see her roll her eyes. She went back to his place right after last call, leaving her car at the bar. Her buzz had worn off over the last few hours, and she thought by the time she got back to her car she would be sober enough to drive. Mostly. Her head was hurting, and she wanted to be hungover in her own bed.

"Yeah, that was, uh, special. I got to get back to my house

so I can feed my cat," she lied. Buster had an automatic feeder. "I'm going to call an Uber. That was so much fun," that part was true. Chris, *(or was it Chad?),* frowned. "Here's my number," she lied again. It was the number to a really good pizza place. She wasn't a complete ass.

Kat wasn't into a relationship right now. Funny how guys always expected her to be. They talked a big game about slaying pussy and putting notches in their belt, but when the chick just wanted a quick fuck, they got all sentimental. This guy seemed to be no different. She almost felt bad for him for a minute, but they had no future. She had tried holding an intelligent conversation with the dude, at least as intelligent as four, *(or was it five* shots?) and more than a few Long Island Iced teas would allow, but this guy had all the intellectual function of a dirty gym sock.

And she certainly would not bring him home to her Catholic mother. Her mom would take one look at this guy and know they were fucking. Sex before marriage was a sin, along with just about everything else. Kat didn't even know if she wanted to marry at all and was close to certain she didn't want any kids. She was already 26, an old maid in her mom's eyes, wasting her uterus. She might even pretend to like Chris, *(Chad?),* if only because it would give her hope that her only daughter might get married and have children, as God intended. Kat wanted nothing to do with that, she also didn't want to break her mother's heart. So, she just gave her stories about guys she was dating, moving goal post after goal post, and blaming it all on just not finding the right guy.

Kat had already broken her mother's heart by leaving the church. She told her she was still a Catholic at heart, (she wasn't) but had her own relationship with God, (she didn't) rendering church unnecessary. She still went to funerals and weddings, *(aren't they really the same thing?)* and knew when to sit, stand, and kneel, but she hadn't been a believer in all that crap since somewhere around 11. None of the dogma made much sense when she applied just a small amount of logic to it. Logic she learned while watching Scooby Doo. The whole mess just unraveled, a revelation she did not disclose to her mother. Kat was always skeptical about a divine creator who didn't seem to do much about all the needless and horrible suffering in the world. Every once in a while she prayed, but had long since stopped expecting any kind of response. Another revelation she kept from her mother, but one that Kat considered a kindness.

Kat picked up her phone and ordered an Uber. At this ungodly hour, right before the sunrise, it would come pretty fast. She got out of this soon-to-be-forgotten guy's bed and tugged on her clothes. He rolled on his side to watch her, still wearing his puppy dog expression.

"Are you sure you can't stay? I make a mean omelet," he said.

So does Denny's. "No thanks, I really need to get back," she said, now feeling a little like a jerk.

Maybe she should give this guy a shot? He was a pretty fantastic lay. Nope, that was the booze talking, he'll get over it and find another girl. Hopefully, one that would share his love of fantasy sports, which she did not. She had already listened to enough of his ranting about his pretend teams or whatever. No, it was better this way.

Kat watched as her Uber got closer, and said, "Almost here, I'm going to go wait outside," she leaned down to give him a kiss on the cheek, a kind gesture really.

As she walked out the door she called to him, "Thanks Chad."

"It's Chris," he called, but she didn't hear him before she closed the door behind her.

Her Uber smelled like beer and the farts of the previous

passengers who like her, probably spent Friday night getting hammered at one local bar or another. Her driver didn't even try to make small talk, and she thought she loved him for it. She got the impression that he had spent the night driving drunks around, hoping one of them didn't puke in his back seat. He seemed relieved that she didn't want to talk either. Both parties were content with the silence.

He pulled up to her car, she tipped him as generously as she could afford, which wasn't generous at all, and the goodwill they had conjured in their silence dissipated. He scowled at her as he pulled away. *Well fuck you too buddy*.

Her car smelled much better than the Uber, but that was about the nicest thing she could say about it. Working her way through college as a waitress left her broke. Well, not quite a waitress per se, but a topless dancer. Pretty close. Same difference really. She was going to be a lawyer, a damn good one too, but tuition was a bitch. She was only going to school part time, so she figured by the time she was 40, she'd be ready to take the bar exam.

She only went back to that guy's place because he had been buying her drinks all night. And because she was horny, there was that too. She had worn a low-cut sweater and skintight jeans, and brought enough money to tip the bartender for a water and an Uber ride home. She never drank on her own dime.

She missed the ignition on the first try, but only because there were two of them. She wondered for only a moment if she should drive, but dismissed the thought. It was so close, and she would take the back streets. Her tight sweater might do double duty to get her free drinks and out of a DUI. If she were to be unlucky enough to get pulled over this time of night. Or morning, as seemed to be the case.

Her apartment wasn't much better than her car, but Buster didn't mind using the litter box on the balcony, so at least it didn't smell like cat box. Her retirement plan included her being the neighborhood crazy cat lady. She was kind of crazy about Buster, a gray tabby with a white Hitler mustache and bib, but he was enough cat for her. At least for now. At some point, a tearjerker of an animal shelter ad would convince her she must save some poor kitten from certain death. With any luck, it would come with a box of wine. But for now, one cat and a huge bag of weed would suffice.

Buster greeted her at the door and wound himself around her legs, hoping to ply her with love to get a can of wet food. His dish was full of kibble, but he was always looking for a bite of the smelly stuff. She picked him up and kissed the top of his head. He tolerated this, but scooted to the pantry, which held the coveted stinky food as soon as he was released. Kat obliged him, while nuking a frozen burrito for herself.

"Looks like we're eating the same thing," she wrinkled her nose at the brown stuff that claimed to be chicken. It resembled the filling in her microwaved burrito. It kind of smelled like it too.

She ate her burrito without tasting it, stripped and climbed into bed. The light was creeping in through the window, and she lay there a moment already comfortable and debating whether to get up and close the curtain. She relented and got up. Buster took the opportunity as an invitation to get comfortable in the warm spot she left behind. She brushed him aside, earning herself a dirty cat look, and snuggled back down. She stared at the ceiling above her and wondered if she should have stayed with Chad. His ceiling was just a tad nicer. She closed her eyes to stop the room from moving in lazy circles, but the sensation stayed with her.

She woke in the late afternoon with a pounding head and a wad of cotton in her mouth. She was supposed to work that night, and thought about calling in. Buster awoke at the foot of her bed, irritated that she had shifted and disturbed him. Soon enough he was snuggling against her face, reminding her that she had an obligation to feed him. To do that, she would need to go to work. She pulled herself from her bed and headed for the bathroom. She showered rinsing the remains of her night with Chad *(Chris?)* off her body.

Kat had left all the notions of sin and Heaven and Hell behind, but the stink of those teachings stuck with her. Lingering like a fart in an elevator. Residual Catholic guilt. Funny, after all those years in church, she wasn't so much worried about being judged by God. Kat figured if there was a god, he wouldn't much care about her sexual exploits, occasional drunkenness *(ok maybe not so occasional)* and a little lie here and there. She thought he would concern himself more with the really serious stuff like murder, rape, or someone peeing on the seat in the bathroom at a concert venue.

The hot water steamed up the bathroom mirror and washed away her thoughts of sin. She liked her life for the most part and would live it as she saw fit. How shitty would it be to spend your one and only life worrying about pissing off a god that might not even be there, only to die and turn to dirt? Let Him judge. She had some sinning to do.

She stepped out of the shower and toweled off. With a couple of hours before she was due to be at work, she turned on the TV and ordered some food. The delivery guy was kind of cute, and she almost considered inviting him in but thought better of it. She didn't want to have to take another shower.

Chapter 2

The parking lot of 'Lil Darlings' was about half full, not too bad for a Thursday night. And Kat went straight to the dressing room, nodding an informal hello to the staff she passed on the way in. The ghost of cigarettes past clung to the walls, leaving the lingering odor of dirty ashtrays in the room. The spilled beer and wads of gum ground into the carpet and upholstery completed the overall ambiance. The dim lighting ensured that even ugly people had at least a shot at looking attractive. She had been here only once during the off hours when it was lit up, a horror she intended never to experience again.

She stepped into the dressing room, which buzzed with gossip about staff and other dancers. The smell was just a little better in here, the most egregious of it obscured with cheap perfume. Glitter coated almost every surface, and Kat had to brush it off a chair before she sat down. It puffed up around her like a sparkly cloud. The shit was like herpes, just when you thought it was gone it would show up in the weirdest of places.

It didn't take her long to paint some muck on her face and be ready for the night. Some girls agonized for hours over their make-up, failing to realize that guys didn't give a shit about whether their eyebrows were on point or not. The low lighting and fake smoke from the dilapidated smoke machine, coupled with the fact that most of the guys got hammered before they even stepped through the doors, made such efforts futile. They were in a titty bar in downtown Portland, for fuck's sake.

Ready for action, she stepped out of the dressing room. Right away, a sweaty guy in an ugly wool suit waved her over. She hated wool suits, as they sometimes gave her little red bumps on her ass. She strode over on her towering platform heels and made small talk for as long as she could stand before she took him back for a lap dance.

It was apparent right away that he had donned the suit in an attempt to look better off than he was. She kind of felt sorry for his pathetic effort, until he stuck his tongue in her ear, slithering inside like a warm slug. She cringed but stayed silent. She pulled herself back to remove his access. First dance of the night, and she could have him kicked out but might lose her tip. Instead, she waited until his eyes were closed and deftly lifted a few twenties from his wallet. She had chosen a spot not quite out of view of the security cameras for exactly this purpose. The song ended, and she didn't bother asking if he wanted another. If he checked his wallet, he would see he didn't have enough money for another, anyway. Pity.

She danced the night away, picking the occasional pocket of the customers who she deemed worthy of the deed. She drove home stinking of used beer and cheap cologne, sparkling with glitter she hadn't applied. Buster once again greeted her at the door, looking for food and ignoring what was already in his dish. Totally oblivious to the fact that he had a date with the vet later that afternoon.

She fed him and poured herself a bowl of Captain Crunch, what she thought of as *human kibble.* She marveled at the sweet destruction of the roof of her mouth. Kat hopped back in bed, thinking she really should shower, but decided she didn't care. Buster took his place at the foot of his bed.

Her phone rang only a few short hours later. Cursing herself for not turning off the ringer, she rolled over to see if she gave a shit who it was. And she didn't. Fearing that her effort was pointless, she tried to go back to sleep. She lay there, forcing her eyes shut. Her hand crept between her legs and started moving. A quick session ringing the devil's doorbell might relax her enough to get back to sleep. After she tried and failed to coax herself back to sleep, she threw the covers off in a huff. She would be tired and pissed off all day.

Buster looked just as irritated, but soon decided it was time to eat. Again. No wonder he was so fucking fat. The vet would undoubtedly bring up his weight at his check-up that was now only an hour away. She would calmly explain to him that she fed him extra meals only under extreme duress and threat of death. Fail to comply and he would surely suffocate her with his ass in her sleep and chew on her soft bits while she was still warm. The vet would listen and then roll his eyes in a stinging indictment of her abilities as a cat mom.

She made her way to the coffee machine, and while it was brewing, she opened another can of cat food Buster didn't need. "Shhh, don't tell the doctor," she whispered to him, he looked up at her like he didn't give a shit what the doctor thought. She could relate. "Yeah, screw that fat shaming son of a bitch."

Coffee in hand, she reached for a stale donut out of the box she had picked up a couple of days ago. She knew that with her 30th birthday lurking in just 4 short years, she would have to give up the donuts. At least if she wanted to keep getting free drinks at the bar. Or she could just find a guy that likes the fatties. She had time to decide. For now, it was all donuts and frozen burritos. She could eat healthy when she was old.

She dunked her donut in her coffee in an attempt to restore some of its moisture. It left little flecks of sugar floating in her thick brew. Along with a few flecks of glitter. She looked at her hand and saw some of the vile stuff clinging to her fingers. She needed a shower.

She checked the time, just under an hour before the vet appointment. She tried to remember where she had put the cat carrier. She dug through her closet, under the sink, which was a stupid place to look, as it couldn't fit. Under her bed. Yet another dumb place. She spent a good 20 minutes looking for the thing before she remembered she had loaned it out. *Fuck.* She looked over at Buster sleeping on the sofa and hoped he wouldn't crawl all over the car on the way there. Or piss in the back seat.

She walked to the bathroom to rinse off the offending glitter and saw that she had run out of time. She pulled her dark brown hair up in a ponytail, tossed on a pair of old jeans, wiped the sleep out of her eyes and decided it was a good thing she looked like a warmed-over sparkly dog turd. At least the vet wouldn't hit on her.

Kat grabbed Buster, who was less than pleased and headed out the door. She deposited the bag of fat and fur into the backseat. "Don't piss in here and I'll get you a can of the extra stinky stuff when we get back," she said. He looked at her as if she were nuts, talking to a cat.

Unconfined, Buster started howling, something he always did in the car. He climbed over the back of the passenger seat and perched on top of the headrest. She couldn't tell if he was terrified or trying to make her crash. He reached out a paw to her side of the car and lost his balance. He clung to the cloth seats with his unclipped claws. Something else the vet would chastise her for. But would happily offer to do for a ridiculous fee. He made his way to her seat and clawed his way up. Howling inches from her ear.

She attempted to dislodge the feline and get him into the back seat, swerving as she turned to the side. She gripped the scruff of his neck, but he was stuck fast, howling even louder. She looked for a place to pull over, but found there wasn't one. Just soft dirt and a few dry patches of grass. This stretch of road was lined with trees, and any place she tried to stop would leave the ass end of her car in the road. She let him go and hoped he would just stay still for a minute. He did not.

Buster reached out with his paw, claws retracted, and batted her wide opened eye.

The surprise of it and not the pain made her wrench the wheel toward the middle of the road. She over-corrected as he smacked her again, this time hitting her cheek. Her assaulted eye was watering, and her vision blurred as her tires hit the gravel on the side of the road. Her depth perception went wonky as the tree swam in to view. She thought she was going to miss it. She was wrong.

The car slammed headfirst into a large Douglas fir. As the air bag exploded in her face, she had just enough time to see Buster smash through the windshield like an overfilled bag of furry jelly with her good eye. She felt her nose burst and heard something that sounded like the cracking of a tree branch, and then only darkness.

She awoke on the ground and opened an eye. The other wouldn't budge, she didn't ponder this development very long as pain riddled her body. She tried to pinpoint it, but it was coming from everywhere. She was aware of a man kneeling next to her. She thought he might be a firefighter.

"It's ok miss. Just lie still," he said.

No worries buddy. I don't think I can move anyway, she thought. Her good eye examined his face. He was damn cute. It crawled over his strong shoulders and broad chest. She was just starting to think dirty thoughts when a disturbing cough erupted from her chest spraying the cute fireman guy with blood. Pink foamy blood. He flinched, but didn't let go.

Frightened, she tried again to move her legs but got nothing. Her arm felt warm and wet, and she tried to bring it up to wipe her mouth, but the pain stopped her before it was much more than a thought. It felt like something was sticking through her arm, or maybe out of it. The sound of the cracking branch replayed in her head.

Buster, she thought suddenly. She tried to draw in a breath to ask about him, but only sprayed the handsome firefighter with more Barbie pink colored bubbly blood.

"It's okay, you're going to be okay," he said, but she didn't believe him. She drew air into her lungs again, but more slowly.

"You're cute, but you're a liar," her voice was tiny. She knew then that she was dying. She wanted to tell him that, but her lungs rejected another attempt at filling up. She closed her eyes and thought of her life.

Our father who art in Heaven, oh what the fuck was the rest? Whatever. God, Jesus whoever, please forgive me for I have sinned. A lot. Like a whole lot. But I swear I believe in your grace and that you died for my sins. I never got the cracker and the wine, but I promise I believe. Please don't let me go to Hell. I've been a pretty decent person overall; I haven't really hurt anyone. I even donated blood a few times. Please, I believe, and I love and worship you forever, I promise.

She wasn't sure if that last part was true, but figured it couldn't hurt. Her thoughts came at her fast as she lay there on the side of the road. She thought of her cat. She thought of all the things she had done in her life. She wasn't sure if any of this mattered at all, soon she'd either be nothing or in Hell.

"I'm dying," she croaked, and there were no more words. Her lungs wouldn't allow any more air and therefore there was nothing to push any more thoughts past her lips. She saw tears in the man's eyes as she closed hers for the last time.

I wonder if I got glitter on him. Was the last thing to cross her mind as her world went dark.

Chapter 3

There was no pain, but there was something odd about how she was standing. There was something off about where she was standing too. She looked down at the white fluffy stuff billowing around her ankles. It was like white cotton candy. No. Like a cloud. She was sort of leaning to one side, as if her body had forgotten how to stand up straight. Kat tried to take a step, and the top half of her body flopped over but then righted itself before she could fall on her face.

There was someone standing in front of her, an elderly lady, so thin that her hospital gown looked as if it hung over a mop. The lady turned to face her, and she gasped, kind of. She couldn't detect that any air had entered her lungs, but she had no sensation of struggling to breathe. The poor woman had dark circles around her eyes, and her cheekbones were sharp points threatening to pierce through her skin.

"What, you never saw a dying old lady before? You don't look so hot yourself, missy," the old lady said. "You look like a third grader's Halloween arts and crafts project." She turned her back to her again.

Kat stared at her, appalled. She had rushed out of the

house, but that was just mean. She looked at her hand and saw it still had some glitter on it. But when she raised the other, she saw that a sharp bone was poking out of her bloody forearm. The sight shocked her, but still no pain. She put her good hand up to her face and touched her nose. Or what used to be her nose. It felt like a crushed snail. Pulpy with hard bits mixed in.

She sensed a presence behind her and turned to look, but her back did that weird thing again. As if, it was no longer one long piece, and she swerved. *Am I drunk?* She didn't think so. *Maybe mushrooms? Ah ha! That makes sense. This is a terrible trip. Maybe acid then.* She was still curious about the person standing behind her and made a more careful attempt at turning around to see him, this time with more success. He gasped when he saw her face.

"Whoa," he recoiled.

That was pretty fucking harsh, she thought. He was 40ish, with graying hair and a small paunch that went just a little past his belt. He looked like a normal dude, if you could get past the fact that half of his skull was missing. Pink and gray brain matter was visible under the cracked shell of his head. She turned back around, deciding that the wrinkled and deflated butt cheeks peeking through the old lady's hospital gown were better to look at. This was no mushroom trip. She was dead.

Ahead of the old lady stood a long line of people. All of their feet disappeared into the wispy white substance in which they were standing. Up ahead in the distance, she saw what looked to be large opalescent gates.

Well, what the fuck do you know? I think I made it to Heaven. She thought about it for a moment and struggled to remember her Catholic teachings. That St. Peter was standing at those gates waiting to judge her life hit her in the face like the air bag had just done. *I think I'm fucked.*

Hell awaits.

She had repented, kind of. At the last minute. Half-assed. But if she remembered correctly, that was a viable loophole. How many killers had found God on death row? She hadn't killed anyone, at least that she knew of. She had slept around and maybe stole a little, but was that really that bad? Well, there was the lying too, but her intentions were good. Ok, maybe not, but didn't good intentions lead to hell, anyway? *I'm totally fucked.*

Kat was afraid. She didn't want to go to Hell. The cartoon depictions of Hell came to her mind, a silly looking dude with a handlebar mustache and a pitchfork surrounded by fire. But the stories of eternal suffering and burning lakes of sulfur that she learned in church drowned out those images. She thought she could handle the cartoon dude. Maybe she could hide a rake in his path for him to step on. Then she'd laugh as the handle came up and smacked him in the face. The priest's visions of hellfire and torture were not as reassuring. The more she thought about it the more she became afraid, and the faster the line seemed to move.

She couldn't see too far ahead, but she figured that not everyone was walking through those gates. The closer she got, the more her terror gripped her. She thought of Buster, who couldn't have survived. Her heart ached for him, but she hoped he got through those gates, or maybe some other gates for animals. She couldn't remember what the church had said about animals. She couldn't feel the physical pain, but her emotions were in full force. Tears filled her eyes, and the line moved even faster.

She struggled to keep her broken back upright as she stepped forward. The old lady was having her turn. She looked up to St. Peter standing at a golden podium. She saw his mouth moving but couldn't hear him talk. It seemed judgement was a private affair. Then the old lady disappeared in a puff of white smoke.

Her turn. St. Peter glanced at her from his perch. He looked down and appeared to be studying something. He frowned, muttering unintelligibly. He looked at her again and spoke in a booming but bored tone.

"You've led quite the interesting life, Miss Kathy."

"My name is Kathryn, actually. Kathryn Louise Robertson to be precise. People call me Kat," she said, offering her best innocent smile.

"Well, Kathy. It seems you were quite the whore, thief, and liar," he said, returning her smile with a smirk.

"With all due respect, I don't think 'whore' actually applies Sir. I did it for free, an act of charity really. And I don't really like being called Kathy," the words didn't sound as helpful as they had in her head. She had once put gum in a classmate's hair for calling her 'Kathy'. She was blowing this, so of course, she doubled down. "I only stole from those who deserved it. And the lies were well intended." *I'm going to Hell. I hope Satan's hot.*

"Stripper, thief and liar. It also says here you were studying to be a lawyer too. We don't have many lawyers here in Heaven," He looked at her over the spectacles balanced on the tip of his nose. The iridescent gates reflected off of his balding head. She might have thought it pretty, if she wasn't so sure she was about to be sent to the pits of Hell. The Catholic version and not the one she saw on Looney Tunes.

St. Peter's frown deepened, "It says here, you repented right before you died. Is that correct? Have you accepted Jesus Christ as your lord and Savior? You haven't stepped into a church in 15 years, and yet as you lay dying you promised to love and worship your divine creator."

"Afraid I might catch fire," she said, regretting the joke in an instant. She was some kind of asshole, making jokes at the gates of Heaven. It was like she wanted to go to Hell. "Yes, of course I have. I have seen the error of my ways. My bad. I love me some Jesus, God, and the holy Casper."

"I can't say that I believe you, Kathy," he smirked. *This dude's a real dick.* "I'd say your rightful place is in hell. Do you know what Hell is like? It is every worst fear you ever had, every pain, every heartache magnified by a thousand for all of eternity. Your human brain can't even fathom the misery you will feel forever." His smirk turned into a malicious grin.

"I was kinda hoping it would be like what I saw on cartoons," she didn't know why she kept talking, or why she couldn't make herself stop. She was not helping her case at all; maybe it was a good thing she had died before becoming a lawyer after all.

"What is a cartoon?" he asked and raised his bushy gray eyebrows with sly curiosity.

Seeing her chance to buy just a little time before her eternal suffering, and maybe even make the case for ignorance she said, "You see cartoons are how I learned about Hell. They are like moving drawings that tell stories to children."

"Huh, a liar even in death. I see that your mother took you to church. You had access to the truth, but chose to ignore it," he smiled again, taking the time to relish catching her in a lie.

"Well Petey," she had given up trying to get through those gates, he was just fucking with her now. "Can't blame a girl for trying," she raised her hand to give him the finger, but the hand dangled awkwardly from her broken arm. Her poor finger just pointed downward.

"You're an insolent little brat, I should send you to the deepest level of Hell this instant," he boomed. But no one reacted behind her. Only she could hear him. He must look ridiculous to those who could see his face, all red and angry. She took a small vindication that she had pissed him off.

Might as well have just a little fun before eternal torture. She stuck out her tongue in the brattiest way she could think of.

"I don't make the rules however, you have repented… technically," he spit the words at her. "You should grovel at the mercy you have been afforded but so obviously don't deserve. God is merciful if you choose to accept Him. You may enter the Kingdom of Heaven, Kathy the whore." At this, she flipped him the bird again, remembering to use her good hand.

He dismissed her with a flippant wave of his hand and one last disapproving look. She was stunned. Then even more so when she did her own disappearing act. One second, she was looking at this dickhead judging her. *Pfft, like he was so great.* The next she was standing on the other side of the gates looking at Heaven.

Holy fuckballs… she made it to Heaven. The first thing she noticed was that her awkward gait was no more. She was standing up straight. Her arm was restored as well. She touched her nose, and that seemed to be alright too. She looked at her skin and saw that it sparkled. But not with stripper glitter. The sparkle was coming from the inside, like it was just part of her skin. Figures she couldn't escape the fucking stuff even in Heaven. Glitter, it seems, is eternal.

Kat was grateful that at least for now, she didn't see anyone else. Her head was spinning and this whole Heaven thing was going to take some getting used to. She looked down and saw that her dirty bloody clothes had been replaced by sparkly robes that flowed over her curves. She would have to see if she could find something more suitable. More fitting, less sparkle. It was Heaven after all, and that should be a simple request.

She touched her hair, which had been dirty and thick with hairspray and fake smoke residue. Now it was silky smooth to the touch and fell around her face in soft waves. She looked around to find a mirror or other reflective surface. As soon as the thought hit her, a pool of sparkling water the color of turquoise appeared. *Does everything fucking sparkle? It's like a divine strip club dressing room.* She kneeled down to look at its surface. She was drop dead gorgeous. Like the best version of herself. A golden circle floated above her head. She reached up to touch and found it was solid.

The water looked cool and inviting and although she wasn't thirsty, she cupped a hand and took a sip. It was like nothing she had tasted, clean and clear. She took another sip and looked up. The old lady who had been in line in front of her was standing on the other side of the little pond. She wasn't old and frail. She was beautiful. If Kat had seen her this way in life, she would not have known that this was the same lady, she bore almost no resemblance to the sickly woman she had seen in line. Heaven had restored her. *Well, this seems pretty fucking cool.*

Buster came to mind along with his last moments. There's no way he survived. If he's here, she needed to find him. He's going to be so pissed. Hopefully Heaven has fancy feast, preferably the salmon pate.

"Buster!" she called as loud as she could and waited. Looking hopefully to the expanse of endless white clouds. When she didn't see him bounding up to her, she tried again. "Buster!"

The not old lady looked to her and said, "You silly girl, cats don't go to Heaven. Dogs do."

Chapter 4

"No cats?" Kat asked the now hot old lady.

"Cat have no souls, they just die. Or go to Hell, I bet." she replied. "I'm Sue, by the way. Thanks for asking." She walked away. Kat hoped she wouldn't run into her again, so she didn't bother trying to remember her name. She's terrible with names, anyway.

This lady had just gotten to Heaven herself. What the hell did she know, anyway? Buster could still show up. Or maybe he had survived? Cats land on their feet, although she wasn't sure that would matter for those that flew through car windshields. But she also thought he could be in an animal Heaven. No, that might suck for him. Maybe just a cat Heaven, where there were slow-moving birds and mice running around and they had their own thumbs to open cans of cat food.

Excitement welled up in her stomach as she looked around again. *Holy fuck. Heaven.* She could hardly believe it. She was still wondering if it was some kind of dream, brought on by copious amounts of drugs administered in the hospital. Could she be lying bruised and broken in a coma? If so, it was one hell of a realistic dream. She wondered how she could prove it to herself. An interesting thought. How does one go about proving that they are, in fact… dead?

The lady had wandered off, but the pond was still there. Kat jumped in. It wasn't cold, nor hot. It was just right. Glorious, in fact. She took a breath as her head surfaced, but no air filled her lungs. But there was no discomfort associated with the lack of air. It just was. She dunked her head back under the water and breathed in. No water filled her lungs either. Cool. A mermaid in Heaven.

She dived deeper and opened her eyes, something she loathed to do in life. It had always been uncomfortable. This was not. She looked around under the surface with as much calm and ease as she had on dry land. There were shimmering stones at the bottom and water blossoms unlike anything she had ever seen. They swayed and moved with the water. Purple and pink petals sitting on emerald green leaves. Fascinated, she had never seen flowers like this ever. If this was a dream, she wasn't in any hurry to wake up.

She had read a book about dreams that had said that you don't dream about people you have never met or seen in life. Sue or something or other, she was certain she had never met or seen. Or at least she hadn't remembered. She was just as bad with faces as she was with names. Many a time she had disappointed a regular strip club customer who had expected her to remember him. One poor smitten specimen she had introduced herself no less than three times. She was more apt to remember a lap than a face. A revelation that he had failed to find amusing. Maybe it didn't really matter whether all this was a dream. If it was, she would just wake up, if it weren't, fuck it. She might as well enjoy it while it lasted. Which she was starting to suspect was going to be an eternity.

She burst out of the pond, flinging her hair backward,

and a shimmering rainbow of water cascaded over her head. She looked around to see if anyone had witnessed this perfect, one might say heavenly, recreation of Arial in 'The Little Mermaid'. No one had. Slightly disappointed she paddled to the side and climbed out. Her robes clung to her, revealing her curves, but there was no cold. No goosebumps or shivers as the air touched her dampened body. She shook off the excess water and tried to decide what direction to go in first.

When she had first popped into this place on the other side of the pearly gates, the ground had been much like it had been as she stood in line awaiting her fate. White and puffy like cotton balls, but as she climbed out of the water, it had transitioned to a more recognizable surface. She suspected the gradual change was intended. So as to not freak the fuck out of the newly dead. *Very considerate.* An unpleasant undercurrent flowed below the surface of that thought. *If they took these kinds of steps to avoid distress, does that mean that distress is possible?* She shook her head to get rid of the thought. *That's just ridiculous, who could be unhappy in Heaven? A totally fucking asshole, that's who.*

Green grass gradually appeared under her bare feet. It was soft and cool as she walked. Trees and other flora appeared in the same way. They seemed to materialize as she got near them. One had fruit on it, and she stopped to check it out. It wasn't anything she recognized, something in between a peach and an orange, maybe. She took a cautious look around. Was this a trap? Eve had fallen for this bullshit, and now all of humanity was paying the price. But there was no talking snake, and it hadn't come with a warning. She reached up and plucked one off the tree. She brought it to her nose and took a long smell. *Fruity Pebbles, it smells just like Fruity Pebbles. Fuck me.* She sunk her teeth into it, and the most wonderful taste flooded her mouth. It did indeed taste like it smelled, but better somehow. She took another bite. And soon she had eaten the entire thing. There were no seeds or hard peel, and it left nothing behind but the juice smeared on her face.

She lifted the bottom of her robes to wipe her mouth and made a curious discovery. She was missing her pussy. The place where it should have been was smooth like a naked Barbie doll. She decided then that she was definitely dead. This was a most disturbing development. Was there no sex in Heaven? An eternity without orgasms? She hiked up her robes even more and explored the blank spot with her hand. There was a slight sensation, but she might as well have been rubbing her elbow. She heard something behind her and turned to see a very handsome young man. She dropped her robes in embarrassment.

"I'm Dylan, pleased to meet you," he said.

Dylan, Dylan, Dylan, she repeated in her mind. Hoping to remember his name. He looked like an angel.

"I'm Kat," she said, and wondered if he could see her blush.

"Welcome to Heaven, sorry you're dead," he said, his halo jiggled suggestively as he spoke. "Well good luck, praise God," he said with an odd smirk.

"Ok, well see you later," she said. As he turned, she noticed the tiny little wings on his back. *Huh? Wings.* She lifted her arm over her head and bent her elbow in an awkward attempt to see if she had her own wings. As far as she could tell, she didn't.

She kept walking, and soon buildings and other structures appeared as the trees had. There had been more trees with other strange looking fruit on them, but she passed them by. Up ahead, a white gazebo crawling with lush green vines. Huge orange and purple flowers hung from them. There were three women sitting and talking inside, and she could hear their excited giggles as she approached.

As she got closer, she saw they were beautiful, but really what did she expect? They all wore robes like hers, but in different colors. Blue, green, and light purple. They also had wings, small sparkly ones, and glowing golden halos. She walked up the steps of the gazebo and they turned to look at her. The one in the blue spoke first, a pale blonde with full red lips and a delicate little nose.

"Hello, you must be new. I'm Lyla," she said.

"I'm Kathryn, but you can call me Kat," she replied.

"I'm Courtney, and this is Tabitha," the redhead in the green said and pointed to the woman in the purple who had dark hair that looked like it might drag on the ground when she stood up. "Why don't you come and sit with us a while?"

"Sure, thanks," Kat walked in and sat facing the three angels. She had much to learn about Heaven. "I have some questions."

"Of course, you do, honey," Lyla said, her words dripping with sweetness. In the strip club, Kat had learned to be skeptical of such a tone. But this wasn't the strip club, she reminded herself.

"Well, first I was hoping to find my cat. He died with me," she said. Lyla smiled at her while the rest of her face stayed perfectly still. Had they been on earth, Kat would have asked her where she got her Botox. It was fabulous.

"There's no need to worry about such things, dear, you're in Heaven. Give thanks to our creator." Lyla said. The smile on her face widened.

"Ok sure, uh thanks, but I would still like to know. He was kind of my best friend, sort of an asshole, but still," Kat said.

"Dogs are man's best friends' silly, praise God." Tabitha piped up. She clapped her hands and whistled, and a large bushy German shepherd came trotting up to the gazebo. It put its head in her lap and stared at her lovingly.

"All dogs go to Heaven," Courtney said. "If you had one

on earth, you'll find it here."

"I was never much of a fan of dogs to be honest. Much more of a cat person," Kat replied. It wasn't like she wished them any harm, but she got slobbered on enough at work. Dogs were needy and clingy. Whereas she found herself flattered when her cat finally paid attention to her. And she could relate, as she too enjoyed a good petting and then to be left the fuck alone.

"If you ask you might be able to get a replacement. Pretty much, like the ones on earth. But not quite. God is great." Lyla said, and Kat thought she spoke like a woman who was quite likely missing her butt hole.

It was time to move on. If Lyla called her *Lovey,* again she would punch her in her impossibly smooth smiling face. Which would probably be a bad move. She didn't think she wanted to find out just yet what happens if you get in trouble in Heaven. Purgatory?

"Thanks, guys, I'm going to check out some more stuff. See you later," She gave them her best *I'm not thinking about punching you in the face right now smile.* But she was totally thinking about punching her in the face.

"Bye! Praise the Lord!" they said in unison.

As she walked away, she thought she heard them whispering in a low tone. *Did I just hear the word whore? I don't even have a pussy.* She brushed the thought aside. She was being paranoid. She had been a bit of an asshole on earth. She just wasn't used to people being nice, and she would have to learn to change her own demeanor. She hadn't even thought there was an afterlife and didn't think in a million years she would make it to Heaven if there was.

Accustomed to backstabbing fake strippers she had not come to Heaven completely empty handed. She had brought some baggage. Still, the interaction unnerved her.

And what was with all the praising? Seemed a tad excessive but then again, they had been saved from eternal torture. A gale of loud laughter erupted behind her. It stopped suddenly when she turned to look. She started to turn to give them the finger but stopped herself midway. *They might not even be talking about me.*

She walked on and saw that more buildings appeared. All muted tones and soothing architecture. Smooth cobblestones rose out of the grass and massaged her feet as she walked. Small cottages stood on either side of the road she walked on. Each one of them unique in their own way but perfectly complemented each other. The slight differences in the colors and shapes of the tiny houses coordinated with the one next to it without giving up their individuality. Heaven had one hell of a planning department. She hoped she would get one of these. A definite step up from her shitty apartment.

There were more people now. Some passed her on the quaint little lane she now walked on, smiling and nodding. She saw a few in their yards and they waved as she passed, smiling back at them. They wore sparkling robes either colored or white like hers, they looked to be in their 20s, maybe 30s. All had halos and most had wings. *Must be a VIP thing.*

Up ahead, past the rows of tidy houses, she saw a larger building. It reminded her of the church she had gone to as a kid. Except without the creepy facade that looked as if it might at any moment swallow her in decaying brickwork and stained glass. The impressive building gave off a cool and calm vibe. Nothing at all like church. The closer she got to it, the more imposing it became. A large stone staircase led up to golden double doors. Above them were the words "Administration".

Chapter 5

Kat hesitated, her hand on the handle. A bit of trepidation bleeding into her excitement. As if, she cheated the system and is now just an imposter in this righteous realm. Did she really deserve salvation? What if she walks in and they tell her that Peter made a mistake, and they send her to Hell? Her hand trembles and she considers walking away. She could just fly under the radar like a kid sneaking into a movie theater. They may find her eventually, but at least she could have a little time in Heaven before she is plunged into the fires of Hell.

She thought again of the teachings of the church. She didn't have too many thoughts on the subject. She hadn't really been paying all that much attention. Her objective in church had simply been not to get in trouble, dead or alive. She had mostly forgotten what she had learned. The one thing that had always stuck with her was that God was never wrong and was always watching and listening. If that were the case then it couldn't be a mistake that she was here, and even if it were, He would already know about it. Right? Unless this was some kind of cruel joke, they were playing on her. A divine prank show devised to entertain the inhabitants of

Heaven. No way is God that big of a dick.

She had so many questions. Even in death, she felt responsible for her damned cat. It was her fault that she hadn't simply canceled the appointment and had taken him unrestrained to end up crashing through the windshield of her crappy car. *Fuck it.* She tugged on the door handle and with a surprising lack of effort, the large golden door swung open.

She stepped into the grand foyer of Heaven's Administration building. It was a vast expanse of opulence and grandeur dripping with elegance. Overwhelmed, she wondered if she had been expecting something that looked more like the DMV. Crowded with lines that never moved full of people with irritated looks on their faces. This looked more like the lobby of a 4-star hotel she couldn't afford. Marble floors, golden candelabras and intricate moldings depicting angels and saints. A deep red carpet stood out in stark relief from the pale marble floor and led to a large counter where a male angel looked to be expecting her.

Anxiety crept back into her thoughts, but his smile was warm and welcoming. He was damned hot too, blonde hair, smoldering eyes, broad shoulders. Her eyes drifted up to the shining halo over his head. She remembered the disappointment she had felt as a kid disrobing a GI Joe and finding a smooth lump where she had been hoping to catch a peek at his junk.

She padded up the carpet, feeling like an interloper with each step. It wasn't like she could just turn around and bolt out the door. That would be rude. At the very least, she might be able to talk this hunky angel into making out for a while. He nodded his gorgeous head in greeting as she approached.

"Hello, Miss Kathy," he said. *God dammit!*

"Hello, call me Kat," she said as gently as she could.

She was not going to spend eternity being called Kathy.

"I'm sorry Kat. St. Peter put it in your file that you liked to be called *Kathy*," he replied. "I'm sure you must have some questions."

"Yeah, that Petey's a real card," she said, and he gave her a puzzled look. "I do have a whole lot of questions. Where's my cat? Plus, I'd love some new clothes, and my…umm" she looked down at her crotch and looked up and blushed a little. She wasn't normally shy about these kinds of things, but then again, she was used to talking dirty to strip club patrons. Asking an angel where her pussy had taken off to was a little out of her comfort zone. Well, a lot out of her comfort zone. The fact that he wouldn't break eye contact wasn't helping either.

"Genitalia is part of the human condition. And you are no longer human. You will be happier without such impure…Um… parts. In Heaven satisfaction and pleasure comes from giving thanks to our divine creator." he said, his serene expression faltered slightly.

"Well, that's a bit of a bummer, but uh thanks again…. God." She said and paused, waiting for the pleasure. But she didn't feel as much as a tingle. She thought his smile widened just a little, but she couldn't be sure, wishful thinking probably. He handed her a slip of paper.

"This will show you the way to your dwelling. It is stocked according to your preferences. The other questions I cannot answer for you. Down the hallway to your right, you will find the one who can help you find the answers you seek, praise Jesus." he said, and his smile grew for sure now. She was instantly suspicious of the gleam in his eye.

"Thank you," she said, and was glad to be free of his piercing gaze. His halo jiggled a little as he nodded goodbye. All this jiggling made her miss her pussy even more.

She nodded her head and started down the hallway. It was lined with closed doors, and she wasn't sure how she would know which one she was supposed to go into. She didn't want to just knock on random doors or walk into one. Who knows what she might walk into? She had passed about ten of them and was about to go back and ask the angel, when she saw one swing open as she neared it. *Well, there you go.*

Butterflies swarmed in her stomach as she neared it. Heaven wasn't at all as she had imagined it. She peered inside, and the humbleness of it compared with the rest of what she had seen surprised her. Simple wood furnishings and plain drapery contrasted sharply with the gold-plated lobby. Candles lit the room, which gave it a sort of mystical vibe. Like a fortuneteller's tent at the county fair. It had a pleasant odor of shaved wood and earth. At the back of the room sat a plain-looking man in simple robes, he had shoulder-length brown hair and kind eyes. Jesus. *Fuck.*

She was about to turn and run when he said, "Come sit my child." With a sweep of his hand, he gestured toward the wooden chair in front of his desk.

Refusing Jesus in Heaven might be a bad idea, so she walked in and sat down. Staring Jesus in the face after living most of her life as an atheist, did little to improve the butterflies in her stomach. They felt like they had acquired swords and were battling to the death.

"I understand you have questions, Kathy," he said. *Great, now Jesus is fucking with me too.*

"I do…sir," she didn't dare correct Jesus. This was like sitting in the principal's office, but way worse. "I really just want to have my cat back and figure out how all this stuff works."

He looked her in her eyes as the angel had done, and she wished he wouldn't. She frowned.

"There is much suffering on earth, but you have been spared hellfire and suffering in death. Your reward is the privilege of Heaven and the chance to spend eternity worshipping your creator and savior. Pretty simple really." he said. *No shit Sherlock,* she thought, and then was terrified he might have heard her thought. "Each must find their own way to the light and knowledge they seek. You have found both." Why she had expected Jesus not to speak cryptically, she hadn't a clue. She was suddenly sure that somewhere there must be a hidden camera and obnoxious TV host lying in wait. Ready to jump out and scream that she had just been punked. Followed by a swift drop through a trap door that led directly to Hell.

"You have been granted a seat with God," he smiled at her.

"That's great. How about my cat? I think he died in the wreck with me. I haven't seen him," she said, thinking she should start small and work her way up to her missing pussy.

"He rests where all cats do. I have seen to it that you are provided a heavenly equivalent," he said, his tone suggested he had done her a favor, while his eyes told her to go fuck herself.

This was getting ridiculous. Her butterflies departed, but a feeling of immense frustration took their place. This seemed like such a simple request, and he was skirting the question like a seasoned politician. Jesus of all people should want to help her. And yet he was dancing around the question like a stripper on a pole. She had to restrain an inappropriate giggle at the thought of Jesus swinging on a stripper pole.

"Thank you, but I really want Buster," she said. He only stared at her. Jesus seemed like a bit of a creep. "Can you tell me where is? I would feel much better knowing he was ok. He's probably mad at me." *Like really super eat my face mad.*

"Go forth and enjoy Heaven Kathy, my child," he said, putting emphasis on the 'Y', lifting his voice and drawing out the sound. *Maybe flipping off St. Peter at the gates of Heaven hadn't been such a great idea. No, fuck that guy. He was a real asshat.*

Feeling defeated she didn't bother asking about her missing lady bits. She rose from her chair, and wondered if she should bow or something. They really should provide some sort of guidance on the protocols of greeting deities, or half deities as the case may be. She decided on an exaggerated head nod, half bow, half catch-you-later, before she turned and left.

She didn't see the hot but weird angel as she exited. Reeling from her encounter with Jesus, she really hoped his dad wasn't poking in her mind at that moment. She left with more questions than answers after talking with the son of God. Go figure, it was just like church.

She walked down the steps and looked at the slip of paper the angel had given her. The directions pointed her clearly down a path to the left of the steps. At least navigating Heaven was easy. It took her down a cobblestone isle much like the one she had passed on her way to the Heaven Administration building. The landscaping reminded her of a TV drama, and everything seemed to shine from within. There were birds singing in the trees and squirrels skittering about. These weren't the souls of the birds and squirrels on earth, but some sort of perfected approximation of them she decided. And dogs. Big ones, small ones. They were everywhere. Heaven must have hordes of pooper-scoopers. But still, she couldn't help but appreciate the loveliness of it all. It was like all the best parts of a warm spring day, without the pollen to gum up her nose.

She came to her own little place and thought that in spite of fucking up her name, they seemed to have gotten this just right. It was like they had plucked it out of her head. And she worried again that they were reading her thoughts. Cream base with moss colored trim and matching picket fence with a jasmine covered trellis at the gate. Roses, gardenias, nestled in a planter by the front door. Kat inhaled deeply, sort of, and the fragrant scent of the flowers filled her head.

A sweet little but sturdy weeping willow sat in the middle of the lawn to the side of the stone path that led to the front door. A rope swing with a wooden seat hung from a branch. She stepped through the gate and sat on the swing. She had no desire to swing, so she just sat and took everything in. Not quite ready to see the inside of the house just yet.

The yard in front of the house to the right of hers is covered in petunias. No lawn, just an expanse of flowers. A bit of flower overkill in her opinion, but she figured it was exactly as the occupant wanted it. Good for them. The house to the left was different. Plain and unadorned, it looked pleasant enough, but something about it felt a little off. To each their own for sure. The door opened and a skinny man stepped out. He had blonde hair, large glasses, a thin mustache and a hollow look to him. If this were his perfected appearance, she would hate to see what he looked like in life. His robes were a drab shade of gray that made his halo glow brighter in contrast. She couldn't see if he had wings or not.

He looked over at her without smiling. He looked as if he was looking through her and into her soul. And she supposed he was. It was her soul that was in Heaven after all. He looked familiar, but she could not place his face. Not unusual for her but she couldn't shake the feeling that she should know who this guy was. He was still looking at her, so she raised her hand and waved hello.

"Hello," he said. His voice was soft and small. "I'm Jeffrey. Glory to the Lord."

Her eyes widened as recognition slapped her in the face. *Jesus Titty Fucking Christ, that's Jeffrey Dahmer.*

Chapter 6

S he brought her hand down in slow motion as if it were moving through water. A look of disgust painted on her face. But there was no way he could be more disgusted than she was after finding out she made it to Heaven only to live next to a serial killer. It seemed getting into Heaven wasn't such a big deal after all.

"Well, fuck you too, Kathy! Not like you're in any position to judge, I heard you were a slut! Praise God!" He yelled before walking back into his creepy little house and slamming his creepy little door. She saw two ugly little wings jutting out from the back of his ugly robe. *Perfect, he's one of the special ones.*

Kat lifted herself up off her swing. *At least he won't be inviting me to dinner.* She cringed. She turned to her own front door, wondering if she could ask to move. Was there any point in it? If that dude is here, how many other killers or rapists were in Heaven too? She certainly didn't think there would be strippers here, let alone serial killers.

She opened her unlocked door. Unlocked because it didn't appear to have one, which given her neighbor seemed to be an issue. At least she wasn't his type. No wonder they didn't like people asking too many questions.

She pushed open the door and for a moment, she forgot all about her creepy neighbor. It was as perfect inside as it was out. She walked in and shut the door. Decorated in muted green and purple tones, she loved the first room she saw instantly. She had a plush sofa that looked as if it was custom made for her butt. She supposed it was. On it sat a black and white cat. Not Buster.

She decided instantly that she would call it Lucifer. A passive aggressive homage to St. Peter and the crappy notes he put in her file. Lucifer hopped down and came to greet her. Purring, it put its front paws on her shins and looked as if asking to be picked up. She obliged. It nuzzled against her face in a disgusting display of affection. As if it wanted nothing in return for its love. Her own cat wouldn't have farted in her direction unless there had been something in it for him.

She carried Lucifer into the kitchen and noticed there was no food or water dish on the floor. She put Lucifer down, and as it walked away with its tail in the air, she also noticed it was missing a butt hole. *Well, that explains the absent food dish.*

Her kitchen was just as wonderful as her living room. It had a small nook which held a table that looked out a bay window and into her yard. Relief flooded her mind that she could not see Jeffrey's house from it. On the table sat a box of donuts, all her favorite kinds. She casually grabbed one out of the pink box and took a huge bite. Not even a little surprised to find it was the best donut she had ever tasted.

She moved to the pantry, where she was once again not surprised to see it was full of her favorite foods. A big box of Captain Crunch sat in the middle of the first shelf, and she tossed her donut in the nearby sink and pulled out the box. She grabbed a handful and stuffed it in her mouth. The cereal did not tear up the roof of her mouth. Not even a little. *Cool.* She had a kitchen window that looked onto the house on the left. Songbirds frolicked in the tree outside the window.

Lucifer followed her out of the kitchen through the living room and into her bedroom. Here it seemed they had taken some creative license. Done in leopard print and deep burgundy with an extremely large heart-shaped bed positioned in the middle of the room. It looked like something straight out of a porno movie. An eternal porn set and no pussy. *St. Peter strikes again. The fucker.* But she also didn't totally hate it. There was a bathroom, but without a toilet. No one shits in Heaven was her conclusion. An enormous bathtub, something she had always wanted but never had in a place of her own, sat in the center of the room. A large sink and vanity occupied the rest of the space. *Sweet.*

A large closet the size of her apartment on earth drew her attention next. She opened the double doors and saw that it was filled with sparkling robes. All slightly different colors. She wondered if Heaven had a mall. Probably not. The closet of her dreams filled with shit she didn't want to wear. *Maybe I'm in Hell after all?*

She dropped the robes she was wearing and took a moment to look at her naked body in the full-length mirror on the wall in her closet. Not a blemish or wrinkle. The scar she got as a kid on her upper thigh from jumping over a fence had vanished. Also absent was the ugly birthmark on her belly. Her skin was perfect, but she found she didn't like it as much as she might have thought. She had grown accustomed to her flaws, and while sometimes they made her a little self-conscious on stage, they made her, well… her.

The closet contained no shoes, but she decided she didn't really need any. She had been walking around barefoot the whole time and nothing had hurt her feet. Nothing hurt at all.

She picked up one foot and looked at the bottom of it; it was as clean as if she had just stepped out of the shower. No bras or shoes needed in Heaven. *So maybe it's not that bad.*

Lucifer had hopped on the bed while she was checking out her closet. She jumped on it too, thinking she would irritate the weird thing, but Lucifer just looked at her with an unconditional love that was so un-catlike. She didn't know if she would want to keep it around.

"Jury's still out on you creepy little fucker," she said. Lucifer just stared at her.

She leaned over to the nightstand and opened a drawer. It held exactly three things, a bible, a rosary, and a gleaming crucifix. As if being in Heaven wasn't a big enough reminder of God's sacrifice of his only son. Which didn't seem to be much of a sacrifice when you consider the dude was only dead for a couple of days, and then went straight to Heaven. Her own nightstand in her shitty apartment had been filled with much more interesting items including a lovely blue dildo called the pool boy. Lucifer was still staring.

"What the fuck are you looking at," she said, and it hopped off the bed and walked out of the room. A cat that listens. How totally fucking weird.

Kat still naked, reached down to explore the strange blank spot between her legs. She had some feeling, a vague memory of the sensation of her clitoris. She began to rub herself. The feeling while subtle began to build. She rubbed more intensely, and reached up to pinch a nipple. She closed her eyes and moved her hand furiously in a desperate attempt at some semblance of an orgasm. She tightened her whole body as the feeling rose slightly. Her calf seized as the ghost of a climax spread from her crotch to her belly. She relaxed her muscles, panting and frustrated.

She pulled on a fresh but regrettably glittery robe and walked back into the living room. Lucifer sat on the sofa, not licking its butt. She frowned at it. She was about to walk out the door when she saw a booklet on the exact coffee table she had eye fucked one time at a Pottery Barn. It had cost about as much as a year's tuition. She sat down on the sofa. It cradled her butt like a kind lover. She picked up the booklet of which the cover read, "So you've made it to Heaven". *Not so hard apparently.* She turned to the first page and read.

When she finished the short book, she had a few answers. For instance, there were days and nights here, but they were more for show than a measure of time. To have only days without the nights might upset sensitive humans. The entire booklet spoke of humans in this way. As if they were fragile, stupid creatures, and she didn't think it was all that far off in that respect. It covered the butt hole thing, mainly that there just weren't any. The genitalia thing was a little more complicated. Considered unseemly, they were kind of like a memory. Wings were a symbol of closeness with God, and could be gained by praising the creator. A little conceited of Him in her opinion. Food was just a pleasure to be enjoyed. Her thoughts were no longer readable here in Heaven, which was a relief. Once saved, there was no longer a need for judgement. All your deepest desires are to be fulfilled. A fact that brought her neighbor to mind. It glossed over just about every other thing she wanted to know. Like how to visit a loved one or where the fuck her cat was. She wondered what the hell God had against cats for fuck's sake.

Lucifer got up and moved to sit in her lap.

"Oh fuck off," she said, and got up to walk out her door. Lucifer fucked off, and laid back down on the sofa to watch her leave.

She peeked out to see if Jeffrey was out there and when she saw he wasn't, she stepped outside. She didn't think he could hurt her, but she wasn't in a hurry to see the dude again.

Her other neighbor was outside. A woman with short blond hair with bangs that hung over one eye and an ample figure. She waved and the woman waved back, motioning for her to come over. Kat walked out of her gate and next door.

"Hi, I'm Kat," she said holding out her hand.

"I'm Karen," the lady said taking her hand. She had the first genuine smile Kat had seen since getting to Heaven. Her hopes soared. "Want to come in and sit for a while? I've been waiting to meet you since your house appeared. I wanted to let you get settled first. I bet your house is awesome." She wasn't wrong.

"I'd love to, Karen," the first person not to call her Kathy and the first one to not creep her the fuck out. She followed the lady inside.

Her house was not Kat's taste, but still lovely. She frowned at the "Live Laugh Love" message embroidered in bright pink and framed above the sofa, but hey, it was her Heaven too. The rest of the walls were covered in crucifixes and crosses. Décor based on an execution device was a tad off putting.

"How do you like it so far?" she asked.

"I'm adjusting, but things are kind of weird," Kat said.

They talked a while. Kat didn't learn anything she didn't really know. There were different Heavens for different religions, but all ruled by the same god. She didn't know about animals. Except to say that the ones in Heaven were like copies of animals, pseudo-animals that weren't quite the same. Except of course for dogs. Like the movie, she saw as a kid. All dogs do in fact go to Heaven. *Go figure.* Why only dogs, God's mysterious way was the only answer she could think of. If she didn't want Lucifer, she could just tell him to go and he would. There was alcohol in Heaven; the priest at her mother's church will be pleased. No weed though, which was bumming her out.

"So, what's up with our neighbor?" Kat asked, it had kind of been the serial killer in the room and it needed to be confronted.

"What do you mean?" Karen's tone darkened.

"Well, he killed and ate people, so why is he here?" Kat asked, not understanding the sudden drop in temperature. They had just been giggling and having a good time. Karen acted like she had just pissed in her Cheerios.

"God grants mercy to those who ask for forgiveness. Who the heck are you to judge? You were granted salvation too," Karen said.

Surprised, Kat knew she didn't want to fuck up this new friendship. She tried to walk it back a little. "Well, I wasn't a saint, but I just figured killing and eating people was a bridge too far."

"And where exactly would you draw the line, huh? My husband was a lazy, cheating son of a bitch, so I cracked him over the head with a cast-iron skillet and buried him in the backyard. The kids missed him, so I buried them with him. Do you want to judge me?" She stood up and made for the door, "I think you should go now."

"Ok, hey I'm sorry," Kat, said. *I'm not though.* The husband she could live with, but this lady had killed her kids too for fuck's sake. She stepped out of Karen's house and into the yard.

Karen was standing in her doorway, and she yelled, "I heard you were a huge slut, Kathy!" then she slammed the door.

"You know what? I was a huge slut, but at least I didn't kill any kids. And my name is Kat!" she screamed at the closed door.

As she walked back through her own gate, Jeffrey was staring expressionless from his doorway. She gave him the finger and went into her own house. Lucifer picked his head up off the sofa, and she gave him the finger too.

Chapter 7

Kat plopped down on her sofa, the cushion enveloping her in the most comfortable way. Lucifer, not at all offended by her rude gesture, hopped up to sit in her lap. Kat petted it, and it began to purr. She thinks it's him, but how the hell would she really know? It has no genitalia. But Buster was missing his balls. So, she decides it's him. Whatever it is, Lucifer doesn't act like any cat she's ever known. He looked up at her, and she softened. It felt good to pet him, even if he made her miss Buster. So far, Lucifer has been the only one not to be a total dick in Heaven. She smiles at the notion. She may keep him after all, but if she manages to find her own ornery feline, she might have to send him away. Then again, maybe not. She looked at his stupid little love-struck face and didn't think she would have the heart.

Her neighbors were psycho killers. She lets that fact sink in a little. Nothing about any of this seemed right, and yet she knew that the whole point of Heaven was to redeem the irredeemable. Maybe she should just lighten up and forgive. She was being pretty judgmental after all. A hypocrite, really. If God could forgive, why couldn't she?

Karen had mentioned booze was here in Heaven. At least

in Catholic Heaven. At least she wasn't raised Mormon. For the first time she could remember, she was glad to have been Catholic, well sort of. She brushed Lucifer off of her lap and couldn't help but be a little disturbed that it didn't bother him at all. He just got up and moved without protest. She made her way to the kitchen. She hadn't checked all the cabinets but didn't really think she had to. She knew everything she would ever want would be there.

She opened a cabinet over the sink and found a lovely bottle of scotch. Like the really good stuff. She looked at the label and it wasn't anything they would have served at 'Lil Darlings. She twisted off the cap and took a long swig. It burned in the most loveliness of ways. Starting a fire in her belly. She looked in the cabinet and saw a tumbler, and she removed it and poured some in. She might be dead, but there was no reason to drink like a slob.

She carried her bottle and glass into the bathroom and drew a bath. Under the sink she found many varieties of bubble bath and bath salts. She picked one out that smelled like gardenias, a fragrance that reminded her of her mom. The scent brought with it sweet memories tainted with melancholy. Kat drained her glass and filled it again.

She gazed down at the bathtub she had always wanted, filled with bubbles and fresh gardenia petals, and stepped in. The water was perfect. She drained her glass again. The scotch was fogging her thoughts, but not really improving her mood. She filled and drained her glass once again. Her brain swimming in booze, her beautiful bathroom started to spin. She closed her eyes, but that only made it spin faster. She thought she might puke. She wondered if she even had a stomach. The sensation became even more intense. She had rocketed past a pleasant buzz and straight into the land of the hammered. She wished she wasn't so drunk.

And just like that, she was sober again. Stone cold sober. She filled her glass again, the bottle of the best scotch still full. She drained her glass and felt her buzz coming on again. Wash, rinse, and repeat. Or, Drink, get drunk, get sober, repeat. She had no idea how long she did this. Her bath water never even got cold. There was a small port window in her bathroom that told her that the sun had gone down. That still wasn't a great indicator of time here. Was an hour the same as on earth? A day? A week? For all she knew, 10 years had passed on earth while she was bathing in scented water and fabulous scotch.

She set the glass down and pulled herself up and out of the tub. She checked her fingers. Not a wrinkle. She toweled off and looked at herself in the mirror. She watched as her hair dried into beautiful waves. In life, it would have taken her at least 45 minutes to get her hair this way. If she could do it at all. She wondered if it would be this way forever. Could she change it if she wanted to? Curly maybe?

Her hair responded to her thoughts and tightened into curls. Amazed, she found she didn't like it, but still. How about short and blonde? In an instant, she had a short blonde haircut with long bangs that swept across her forehead. *Eww, a Karen do*. It sucked, but there it was. She played for a while, trying out different hairstyles and amusing herself. Make up too. She went smoky, casual, and dramatic. Fun for a little while, but became boring.

Was it dinnertime? Was she hungry? Not really. She headed into her kitchen and willed a steak. It was delicious, but without a real appetite, the satisfaction was sort of superficial. Crème brûlée? Sure. Boston cream pie? Of course. Without being hungry and with everything on demand, it made everything a little less special. Well, not special at all really. When she was a kid, and her dad was still alive, he had taken her to Disneyland. She left the park exhausted and sticky, but with a head full of joy, she told him she never wanted to leave. She wanted to live there. He told her she would get bored, it wouldn't be special if she were there every day. And she had thought he was an idiot.

She padded back into her bedroom. She hadn't dressed after her bath. Why bother? The temperature was perfect in her new home. She tested that and willed it cold. And then she could see her breath. Then back to perfect. She jumped on her bed and opened her nightstand drawer. She pulled out the bible and flipped through the pages. Which was more than she had done during her whole life on earth. What a strange book, full of awful and fantastical stories. Most of it left to be interpreted by mere mortals; you'd think if God didn't really want anyone to go to Hell, he'd have been a little clearer in his texts. "A guide to your eternal soul… for dummies" would have really done the trick.

Chris, *or whatever,* crossed her mind. Maybe Heaven's nightlife would have something to offer. Were there bars in Heaven? She must have drank a gallon of fine scotch but felt no ill effects. That has to be something to be happy about. All the booze and no hangover or puke to find in the morning. She was really going to have try to look at this place with a glass is half full type attitude. In fact, it was never even empty.

The night was cool, but comfortable. She walked down her street and looked up at the stars. She had loved the night on earth, but she learned none of the planets or constellations while she was alive. She didn't know if they were the same or not. The moon hung huge in the night sky. It didn't resemble anything she had remembered on earth. She tried hard to think about what a full moon had looked like. The memory was there, but faded. Like a photocopy.

She pictured her mom too; the memory of her face had become just a little fuzzy. A little less there. Was she going to lose the memories of her life? That thought saddened and scared her. She thought maybe when she got back that she would write the memories of her life. A postmortem memoir. Something to help her hang on to her memories. She couldn't be sure that they would fade away, but she didn't want to chance it. She wondered if everything here was a facade of sorts.

Up ahead she saw a glow of lights coming from a building. She could go for a drink. Again. A joint would be better though. It was a large open aired covered patio with lights hanging from the rooftop. There were sofas and tables situated around a marble bar. In the middle sat every kind of alcohol she had ever encountered, plus a whole lot more. She saw haloed people milling around inside, holding various types of glasses. Laughter and conversation poured out and into her ears. It sounded like fun. A lot of fun. She walked faster.

The sounds and the lights were inviting. Kat thought maybe she could meet someone worth hanging out with. Karen had left a terrible taste in her mouth. Maybe a guy or something even? Someone to share that huge bed with, if only for a little while. Someone to talk to. A relationship even. It took death for her to get serious. She smiled at that. She was almost running now.

She stopped dead. Well, she just stopped. She was already dead. The blond angel *Lyla?* she had met in the gazebo caught sight of her and motioned to her cohorts. Soon all the chatter and laughter stopped, and they all turned to look at her. The silence bored right through her. The angels cupped their hands around their mouths and whispered. Their tone was low but meant to be heard.

"She flipped off St. Peter. Slut. Whore. Praise God's

forgiveness." the words attacked her. The low tone doing nothing to soften the sting.

Jeez, that's pretty harsh. Heaven is full of assholes. Figuratively speaking. She turned around to leave. Her thoughts turned to Jeffrey next door. She wasn't anywhere near as bad as that dude. Just a little loose really. Did they treat him this way? He had repented and been saved, just as she had, and had earned his reward.

Disappointed and more than a little pissed she walked on. She was in no hurry to get back to her place. The night was pleasant and there was a slight breeze that carried the scent of flowers. She still had hope that maybe there was someone else here that would help her abject loneliness.

Kat was looking for new people in Heaven. Maybe she should be looking for people that were already here. Weren't you supposed to be with your loved ones? Now she felt kind of dumb. Why was she dicking around with looking for other people? When there might be people here she knew already.

She hadn't known many people who had died. Her heart sank, but just a little. Then she remembered her dad. She was so young when he passed. Not long after the trip to Disneyland her mom rushed him to the hospital where he died of a heart attack. She always thought that her father mostly humored her mother when he went to church. But she thought he probably made it to Heaven.

Now why wouldn't the angel at the Administration building say anything? Of all the fucked-up things. She was just about over trying to figure out how things really worked here. It all seemed designed to be confusing, or at least misleading. Jesus hadn't been any help either. He spoke without saying much of anything at all. *Go forth and enjoy Heaven.* Blah blah blah. What the hell?

She reached her door and saw Karen sneering from her living room window. *Stuff it, you horrible bitch.* She walked inside and sat on her sofa. Lucifer looked at her with his odd love. She looked for the booklet, but it seemed to have disappeared. She didn't remember reading about how to find loved ones here. She was sure she could, though. Maybe she needed to go back and talk to the hunky angel. Was the Administrative building closed now? Could she just will the knowledge?

She pictured what she could of her dad. Not much really, she remembered him more from pictures. She got up and went to her kitchen, thinking a cup of tea would help her think. It used to anyway. A cup of chamomile appeared on her counter; she picked it up and relished a sip. She sat down at her table. *Ooo, donut!* She took one and almost dunked it into her tea, but then remembered she would probably never eat a stale donut again. The thought made her just a little sad until she took another bite of the Heaven donut.

First thing in the morning, she would go back to the Administration building to ask how to find her dad. She wondered if she should go to sleep. She wasn't tired, but she had loved to sleep. As she had that thought, her eyelids grew heavy. A rest for her mind sounded nice. She walked into her room; Lucifer hopped off the sofa and followed her. She stripped out of her robe, and it crossed her mind to brush her teeth. She giggled out loud. There was no toothbrush. If you didn't poop in Heaven, you probably couldn't get cavities or bad breath either. She snuggled under the covers and Lucifer crawled up next to her. She closed her eyes and dreamed of her life on earth. She dreamed of her mom, the awful guy in the wool suit, Chris/Chad, and Buster.

Chapter 8

Light poured through the window and flowed over her face. Like sunshine bukkake. Disappointed to wake up in Heaven, Kat sat up in bed. As she drifted off to sleep, she thought she might wake up in her old shitty apartment, and all this was just a weird dream. No such luck. She tossed off the covers and got out of bed. She went to the bathroom and saw that her hair was perfect and there were no dark circles under her eyes, which should have been a given with all the whiskey she drank the night before.

She was going to find her dad today. She went to her closet and picked out a pale mint green robe at random. Kat hadn't seen her father in 20 years, and she did not know what to expect. Would he recognize her? She was sure he would, he must. Her halo bobbed up and down stupidly as she moved her head to check herself out.

Lucifer took his spot on the sofa and watched her move around her little house. She had some coffee and a donut, more out of habit than to ward off sleepiness and hunger. Doing these little things made her feel a little better about being here. She glanced out the window. She saw Karen in her yard smelling her petunias and recoiled a little.

Kat stepped out of the door and waved a cordial goodbye to Lucifer, who had not once tried to trip her by weaving in and out of her legs. She was getting a little attached to the strange creature who looked like a cat but didn't act like one. The day was beautiful, and she wondered if it ever rained in Heaven. She hoped it would. The sunny spring like weather was nice, but she enjoyed a good thunderstorm.

There was no sign of the cannibal serial killer next door, so that was good. Everything was nice on her walk to the Administration building. Which wasn't so much nice as eerie. As she walked, she thought she might understand how people could forget their lives. To dismiss the worries and concerns of those on earth. She knew that when her time came, her mother would love it here. At least she would if she were lucky enough to have a place not neighbored by killers. Kat thought she had brought much of her fate in Heaven on herself. She had been a bit of a turd to St. Peter. She would have probably done the same thing had she been in his shoes. In her defense, she really didn't think he was going to let her in at all. She was getting her just desserts and donuts. *My lord, the damn donuts.*

She passed a few of the other occupants in Heaven, and they smiled and waved. None of them attempted to talk to her or greet her. She thought that was just as well. She still thought that might change. Finding the people which she had a connection to on earth would be a good start. Maybe her dad could explain things better and help her get along here. If she remembered correctly, he had been good at explaining things.

The Administration building shimmered in the heavenly light, and she didn't pause at the front doors as she had the day before. She now knew what to expect. The handsome angel stood at the large counter as he did the day before. He smiled at her as she approached, and she thought he had lost some of his appeal. The encounter with the gaggle of angels last night had jarred her. They seemed to relish in their contempt of her, and she saw this one as part of the same group.

"Hello, again," she said.

"How can I help, Kathy?" he replied, smiling at the frown that appeared on her face.

"My father passed over 20…" she paused, "20 earth years ago, and I would like to see him."

The angel looked down at something on the counter and produced a piece of paper like the one he had given her to find her own dwelling. He handed it to her.

"Here you go, but you should know, people can be different here than you may remember on earth," the angel said.

"I was only 5 when he died, I don't remember much anyway, but thank you," Kat said, wishing again that he would break eye contact for just a second. It was exhausting, all this staring.

"I suggest you speak with Jesus before you seek your father," he said.

She thought of her encounter with him the day before, and couldn't imagine that he would provide any more clarity on the matter.

"I'm good, but thanks again," she said and turned away and walked toward the large double doors.

"Anytime, Kathy. Praise God." The angel called to her back, and she rolled her eyes.

"Uh yeah sure. Praise God and thanks for the donuts."

The sun shone in her eyes as she stepped out the double doors, and she wished she had sunglasses. They appeared on her face. Nice. She looked at the paper the angel had given her and followed the directions written there.

A lingering sense of deception seemed to lurk beneath the

surface of this place. Not everyone spoke in riddles like Jesus, but she felt like there was a kind of holding back of information. Not lying, but withholding. Everyone acknowledged her questions, but the answers were sketchy at best, if she got any at all. It was the same as on earth. Just trust God's plan. Don't look too deep. Knowledge is dangerous while faith is revered. Even after death, answers were elusive.

Still, she enjoyed the environment, and had gotten so lost in thought, she almost missed her dad's house. She checked her paper. Although she didn't really need to, she simply knew it was his. She doubted if she had even needed direction at all. Maybe it was just a newbie thing and once she had grown accustomed to the idiosyncrasies of Heaven, she would just know.

Her father's place was simple, almost like Jeffrey's next door to hers, but without all the horrible death and cannibal vibes. Built much like hers, but with a simple lawn and painted in earth tones. There was a small oak tree in the middle of the yard. A little red brick pathway led to the door. She walked up to it and knocked, suddenly a little nervous. *What if he heard all the shit the angels talked?*

The door opened and a very young version of her father stood in front of her. He was tall, and had piercing blue eyes, which she had not inherited, but with the dark hair that she had. She could see the recognition in his eyes. They embraced. Her eyes filled with tears that didn't spill over. After some time, he released her. She could smell alcohol on him, scotch maybe. She smiled.

"Kathryn," he said. "Look at you, you're beautiful."

"You're looking pretty well yourself for a dead guy. I wasn't sure I was going to recognize you. But that seems not to be an issue here. Dad, I'm having a tough time figuring all this out," her tears came again, but stayed in her eyes. She suspected they would never spill over. There was sadness in Heaven, but no tears.

"Come in, I'll see if I can help. But I've got to warn you, I don't think I've figured it out myself," he looked at her up and down. "It is so good to see you. I mean, terrible that you're dead, but still really good to see you."

She saw tears in his own eyes as he welcomed her inside. His home was humble, but comfortable. There was a bottle of the same scotch she had been drinking along with a short glass on the coffee table. They both sat down on his very dad-like plaid sofa, and he motioned to the bottle.

"Would you like some? Praise God." he asked while looking around. She thought about it and almost declined. But what the hell, why not?

"Sure," she said, and a second glass appeared next to his. He filled it a quarter of the way, as he filled his own about half. Her heart swelled. Such a dad move. "Thanks."

"How long have you been here?" he said. "They don't inform you when a relative comes in. Not sure why not."

"A day or two, still getting used to the time here. It feels different. A little disorienting. I was in a car accident. Kat said.

"Shit, how long have I been here?" he said, with genuine curiosity.

"I was 5 when you died, 21 years ago. Mom always said you were looking down on us from Heaven," she said.

"Oh, your mother. I almost forgot about her. I think she's the reason I'm here. Not that she killed me. My damn heart did that, but that I thought to repent right before. My memories of my life are strange. I only have the bare bones of it all left now. Frankly I'm surprised I remembered you." He looked pained. "I'm sorry. I didn't mean to hurt your feelings. But memories get all blurry when you've been here awhile. I can barely keep track anymore." He took a long drink, filled his glass and took another long drink.

"I've started to notice that. Dad, I'm not sure I like it here. Some of the angels have been real jerks and Jesus doesn't make sense, and I know I pissed of St. Peter. Mom is why I'm here too. I was an atheist pretty much but remembered to say a prayer as I died on the side of the road," she tried not to ramble but couldn't help it. The relief of finding and talking to her dad bubbled over and spilled out of her mouth.

A dog sauntered into the living room and laid down at her father's feet. It looked up at him with loving eyes, just like a real dog. She didn't bother to check to see if it had a butt hole, she already knew it wouldn't.

"That's Beelzebub, I call him Bub for short," her dad said and reached down to scratch his head. Bub looked delighted. "Yeah, angels can be dicks. They remind me of your mother's church group. Lousy bunch."

"I can't seem to make any friends, dad. And I miss my cat." She said.

"Me either. But then I found this bottle, and I guess I just forgot," he took another long swallow.

His words were getting fuzzy and tears that never fell stood in his eyes. Kat took a long sip of her drink. She was happy to have found her dad, and even more happy to have found him so much like her, or vice versa.

"It's ok dad. I know it is Heaven, but things seem pretty fucked up here. It's not your fault. I'm going to keep trying," Kat said. She took a sip of her drink and watched him drain his glass yet another time. "Do you know anyone else here?"

He thought for a while, a long while. He didn't seem to be interested at all in getting sober again. Kat thought he must just stay drunk, and she really couldn't blame him.

"Oh! My sister! I saw her a while ago, we hung out, but then we kind of just kept to ourselves. I think I can help you find her," he said.

His words were a mash of syllables that were getting harder to decipher. She remembered having an aunt that had died not long after she was born. She had been a bridesmaid in her parents' wedding, and she remembered seeing a photo of her. Aunt Judy.

"That's great, dad. I'd love to talk to her. Do you want to come with me?" She hoped he would say yes.

"Uh, I think I'd rather stay here if you don't mind," he slurred.

He reached into a drawer in the coffee table and pulled out a slip of paper. He closed his eyes, and then handed it to her. On it were directions. She looked at the drunken scribble, and it made her sad. She promised herself she would visit him often, but part of her thought she might just end up looking for the bottom of a bottle that didn't exist. She got up to leave. Eager to find Aunt Judy. Her dad stayed on the couch, his hand on Bub's head.

"Bye dad, I'll be back soon," Kat said as she opened the door.

"Goodbye, Kathryn." he said.

Chapter 9

K at stepped back out into the daylight, but it had grown darker as she talked with her father. White, gray, and silver clouds swarmed the sky, and she could smell the oncoming rain. She wondered if her earlier thought of thunderstorms had brought it on, or if it was just another way for Heaven to make things a little more earthlike. The temperature had cooled slightly but not enough to bring a chill.

She walked along the path written on her father's note. Happy to have found him, but she was alarmed that he spent all his time with his whiskey. Not even the thought of visiting his sister along with the daughter he hadn't seen in 20 years was appealing enough to pull him out of that bottle. It made her even more determined to find her aunt. Heaven was confusing, and she was just about convinced that it was intentional. She was sure that all the booze and donuts masked a larger truth. She didn't know what it was, but she really didn't want to spend eternity getting drunk and trying to masturbate.

A big fat drop of rain surprised her when it hit her in the middle of her head. The atmosphere was electric, and a rumble of thunder shook the trees. She stowed her sunglasses, and now she wanted an umbrella. It appeared unopened in her hand. The rain came faster, but she allowed it to fall on her for a few moments before she opened her umbrella. She felt the dampness touch her robe, and for just a minute, it made her feel alive again.

As had had happened before, she became lost in her thoughts as she strolled in the rain. It was easy to do here. The rain hit the leaves on the trees with a sound that hypnotized her. The sounds and the smells were calm and so pleasant that she didn't just miss her aunt's home. She had gone about a mile past it. When she realized it, she had the same feeling like it had been deliberate. As if Heaven rather she didn't. Get lost in the place's magic, the booze, or the donuts. *Go forth and enjoy Heaven, my child,* Jesus spoke in her head. Go forth and enjoy, and don't bother with anything else. Except tonguing God's ass of course. *Praise God.*

Kat didn't know her aunt in life, but looking at her house gave her the first clue of who she was. She thought they might be friends. Aunt Judy's house was an aggressive shade of purple with white trim. Snapdragons and birds of paradise filled her yard, a whimsical but odd combination. There was a small porch, which held a bench swing for two. Sitting next to it was a little table, and on that sat an ashtray, a lighter, and a pack of unfiltered Lucky Strikes. Kat was going to like Aunt Judy. She had a gate at the entrance to her yard but no walkway to her door. Kat opened the gate and tiptoed through the snapdragons so as not to crush them. As she did, she thought herself a little silly because of the certainty that even if she were to smash them all, they would just right themselves again. You can't kill a flower in Heaven.

Kat knocked lightly on her Aunt Judy's door. She

wasn't as nervous as she had been at her dad's house. When the door opened, a very pretty woman answered and without a word put her arms around her and held tight. When Aunt Judy finally let her go, she held on to her shoulders and looked Kat up and down. "You're Dave's kid, I can tell." She pulled her in close and gave her a huge wet smack on the cheek, leaving a large wet lipstick stain. Kat didn't mind at all.

"Come in, come in. I haven't had a visitor in ages," she said.

"I'm Kathryn, or Kat," Kat said and looked at her aunt.

"I know silly. I'm dead not stupid."

Aunt Judy was a short lady, but her presence was towering. She had light brown hair that hung in a braid down her back. She had been in her late 40's when she died, but in Heaven, she looked to be in her mid-twenties. Her robe was a shimmering shade of burnt orange.

"I know, I had forgotten, but seeing your face just now reminded me of holding you shortly after you were brought home," she said, as if Kat already knew this fact. "I helped pick out your name. You were named after your grandmother, she's not here by the way," she whispered this last part while cupping her mouth with her hand. "Don't just stand there staring, come in!" that part she said loud enough for all of Heaven to hear.

Kat stepped through the doorway and into a sea of cats. Something like 10 or 12, but they were all milling around and impossible to count. They all looked up at her in unison with the same loving face as her Lucifer.

"They aren't quite like real cats, but they bring me joy and I love them anyway," Aunt Judy said.

"I have one too. I named him Lucifer. My cat died in the car wreck with me," Kat said.

"Lucifer! You're alright my girl," Judy beamed at her and began to wade through her cats and into her kitchen.

Kat had to tip toe through cats as she had with the snapdragons to follow, amazed by the fact that the whole place didn't smell like a litter box. Judy's place looked like something out of a 70's era gameshow set. Bright colors and abstract flowers, the loud décor was not as unpleasant as one might expect. Better than a room full of crosses, although Aunt Judy had a few. Kat found it charming in spite of the fact that every color seemed to clash with the one next to it. Bright blue and orange somehow found harmony with the pale pink and neon green. It should have looked like a big mess, but it was all lovely somehow.

"Come sit, Love," Aunt Judy commanded, and Kat did as she was told.

"Thank you," Kat said, and noticed a pink box on the little kitchen table, Judy saw her looking.

"Danish, would you like one? They never get stale or run out. I thought I would get sick of them, but nope," Judy said, and opened the box and took out one that looked to be cheese and raspberry.

Kat took out one that appeared to be apricot, but as she took a bite, she noticed it was the same fruit she had tasted from the tree. Pleasure filled her mouth, and it was almost as good as her donuts. She thought the only thing she needed was a cup of coffee. A steaming mug materialized in front of her.

"Isn't that pretty great?" her aunt said around a mouthful of Danish.

"I have one with donuts," Kat said.

"Can you keep a secret?" Aunt Judy said, in a quiet tone that seemed out of place in the decoratively loud kitchen. She didn't wait for an answer. "Look what I have. You can't just wish for this stuff. You have to know someone."

Aunt Judy reached her hand under the table and

brought out a large turquoise glass bong. Judy had a maniacal smile as she set it on the table, then reached into her robe pocket and pulled out a large plastic baggie of weed. Kat liked Aunt Judy a lot.

"This stuff doesn't come from Heaven. I don't think you can get in trouble for it though, I'm not sure anyone even knows about it. Other than the guy I get it from and now you of course," Aunt Judy said, and she opened the bag and waved it under Kat's nose.

"That looks even better than the donuts," Kat replied.

Judy packed the bowl on the bong stem and passed it to Kat. Kat lit it up and took a long pull off it. When she blew it out, she expected to be racked with rough coughs, but none came. Missing her lungs had its advantages. The weed hit her head like a ton of bricks. Harder and faster than the scotch. Her aunt was going to have to drag her out of her house, Kat never wanted to leave. Judy repacked the bowl and lit it herself.

"It comes from Hell," Judy whispered. "There's a rip in the fabric of Heaven, or something deep in the forest out by the waterfall. I was exploring not long after I got here and heard a weird sound coming from a bunch of rocks. When I got close to it, this little dude with the face of a wolf. He's hideous. His name is Amon, and he's a demon. I've been smoking this stuff for…. well, I don't know how long. But the only thing he wants for it is some of that orange fruit. Have you tried it? It's delicious," stoned, Aunt Judy was rambling, and Kat hung on every word.

"I don't think he can come up out of that hole," Aunt Judy continued. "He told me some stuff about Hell. I'm not sure I can believe him though. I mean Hell is full of liars, right?"

"I think Heaven is full of liars too. I live next door to Jeffrey Dahmer for fuck's sake. How the fuck did he get here?" Kat said with a mouth full of cotton. She needed some water, and there it was.

"Forgiveness, same as you, I'll bet. Praise the Lord. Who the hell is Jeffrey Dahmer, Love?" Judy asked.

"He's a serial killer who ate parts of his victims," Kat answered, her lip curled in disgust.

"God works in mysterious ways. His greatest gift is salvation," Aunt Judy's voice was barely above a whisper, and Kat thought she sounded more than a little frightened.

"I saw my dad… he likes his booze. But everyone else here has been kind of an asshole," Kat said and felt bad about it saying it, but it was the truth.

"Well, would you rather be in Hell?" Aunt Judy said as she grabbed another Danish.

"I expected to be in Hell… Well, I just expected not to be anywhere anymore. But I guess I thought Heaven would be about hanging with your loved ones who had passed. That everyone would be nice. That doesn't seem to be it at all. I understand the forgiveness part, but does that mean that good people who didn't repent are in Hell?" Kat said.

"I think it does, Love. If you remember, salvation is about accepting God and not so much about your earthly deeds. For the sacrifice of Jesus to be fully rectified, sinners must accept it. And for that to happen, they have to sin. There are many non-believers in Hell that weren't bad people in their lives. At least that's what Amon told me. He told me that in Hell, people just are who they were. There isn't the fire and flames of eternal torture. He said there is pain, but also pleasure. He says the souls there get justice and if they were kind on earth, they are treated kindly in Hell. It seems to counter what I had learned about Hell. I'm afraid he says that stuff to trick me into going into Hell. He is a demon, and I don't trust him. I wonder if it is still possible for a redeemed soul to get kicked out of Heaven. It happened to Satan," Aunt

Judy looked uncomfortable in her seat, and she refreshed the weed in the bowl and lit it without offering it to Kat first.

Kat sat and tried to process what her aunt had told her. She wanted to meet this Amon and judge for herself. Aunt Judy's demeanor had gone dark, and she was afraid to press her any further about it. She finished smoking and offered no more to Kat. Kat took this as a sign that their visit was ending. She had a lot of stuff to think about. As much as she wanted to know more, Kat thought it best that she go back to her place. She would come back and hopefully get some more information about Amon later.

"Thanks, Aunty. That was so much fun. I'm going to head back to my place. I'll come back to visit. Maybe you can show me how to find your little demon friend?" this last part she hadn't meant to say out loud, and she winced as she heard it come out of her mouth. *Fuck.*

"No! Demons are dangerous and I will not be responsible for sending you to Hell! I shouldn't have told you," Aunt Judy's anger flashed.

"I'm sorry, I didn't mean to upset you," Kat tried to repair the damage, but the look on Aunt Judy's face told her that wasn't possible. At least not yet.

Kat stood up from the table with her head still foggy from the weed. The cats parted to let her through on her way to the front door. They seemed to be ready for her to leave as well. Aunt Judy stayed seated.

As she opened the door to leave, she heard her long dead aunt say, "Be careful Kathryn, our God is merciful, but has a vengeful side."

Chapter 10

Dark clouds still cluttered up the sky, but the rain had stopped falling. There was a rainbow arching over the dampened landscape. Everything looked fresh, so pretty much like it looked before it rained. The birds and squirrels that had hidden from the storm came back out in droves. They splashed and played in the clear puddles, and for a moment, Kat forgot the disturbing end of the conversation with her Aunt Judy.

Her aunt sounded as if she had been afraid of God. A loving, merciful god shouldn't be something to fear in Kat's opinion. And the whole vengeful part was the most fucked up. She remembered some stories of the bible she learned as a kid. The god of those stories seemed like a dick. He set up this entire system of sin and redemption and punishment. As she got older, she discounted everything she had learned, if only because it went against her own developing sense of morality. She was far from perfect, but at least she hadn't drowned the whole world. She rejected all of it. God, the bible, and all the rest. That she repented at the last moment of her life was a reflexive action that she hadn't meant at all. Just the ramblings of a dying brain. It seemed wrong that she got into Heaven on a technicality. Living next door to one of the most prolific and vile serial killers in Heaven confirmed that supposition for her.

But did she really want the alternative? That was the harder question for Kat, and one she was trying to work out in her head as she walked. She hadn't been the best person in life. She was promiscuous for sure, but was that really so bad? Was she really thinking she would rather be in Hell? That didn't make much sense either.

If there was anything she might have felt bad about doing in her life, it might be the stealing. Definitely not all the sex. God made it feel good, how could he possibly punish her for that? But even those never resulted in anyone being hurt. She didn't steal enough to ruin anyone's life. She didn't think she belonged in Hell for those things.

She had been walking for a while, thinking about all this stuff for some time. She wasn't sure what time it was, but the sun was lower in the sky than it had been. Her legs never tired, and it seemed so easy to get lost in her own thoughts. Her little home had everything she had ever wanted or could ever need, but there was something about strolling around this strange but beautiful place that she found hypnotic.

She wasn't worried about getting lost. She had no doubt that when she was ready to go home that she would know the way. It was her place where she was meant to be. *He wants us to be there, to forget our lives and spend eternity with the things we found pleasure in on earth.* Memories fade and are to be forgotten. Ahead she saw something that brought her out of her thoughts. Someone standing on a platform speaking. Jesus.

The people standing around the little stage looked to be enthralled with his speech. His mannerisms gentle, he moved his hands with his words in a smooth gesture that was easy to watch. Kat stepped closer as quietly as she could. She did not want to invite the scorn of the angels again, but she also wanted to listen.

"Ask and it will be given to you; seek and you will find; knock and the door will be opened to you. For everyone who asks receives; the one who seeks finds; and to the one who knocks, the door will be opened. But seek first his kingdom and his righteousness, and all these things will be given to you as well. I am the way, the truth, and the life. No one comes to the father except through me. 'Love the Lord your God with all your heart and with all your soul and with your entire mind.' This is the first and greatest commandment." Jesus said in a voice that was soft, but loud enough to be heard.

The spectators bowed their heads and mumbled "Amen" in unison. To Kat, they looked like they had been drugged. Their faces placid and emotionless. She had to wonder if they understood what he was saying or if they even cared to. The first commandment was to love the lord. Why would you want to love the guy who created disease and Hell? She was starting to think this was some sort of set up.

Standing close enough to the stage to catch a guitar pick or flash her tits was the blond woman from the gazebo. Lyla. She turned to look at Kat, her eyes the color of ice chips. If looks could kill, she would have been dead. Or not, she was dead already. Lyla turned to the person standing next to her, a tall dark and most assuredly dick-less guy but was speaking too softly for Kat to hear. They both stared at her as they talked. The talk spread through the crowd, and soon all of them had turned from Jesus to stare at her. The whispering became louder, but Jesus had yet to notice. He babbled, oblivious to the fact that no one seemed to pay attention. Kat got the impression he was happy just to hear himself talk.

"In the same way, let your light shine before others, that they may see your good deeds and glorify your Father in

Heaven." He said, loud but monotone.

"Hey maybe you fuckers should listen to that guy?"

The angels threw their collective hands to their throats as if they had been attacked. As if they hadn't been the ones doing the attacking in the first place. Jesus went on as if nothing was happening.

"Do you even belong here Kathy the Whore? You should go back to your house and let the righteous enjoy the fruits of Heaven," Lyla said in a singsong voice. The others nodded their heads in agreement.

She knew there was a perfect response here, several probably, but in her intense anger and a little embarrassment if she was being honest, all of them eluded her. She had heard once that if you encounter a Mountain Lion in the woods, you should make yourself appear taller to scare it away. Kat stood on her tiptoes, an effort to be a little more intimidating, and flipped them off with both middle fingers. She stuck out her tongue for good measure, before turning around and heading for home. She hoped that none of them saw the tears in her eyes as she did. She knew that no matter how much she felt like it, her tears would never make it past her eyelids.

She stomped back home, angry and hurt. She didn't understand why everyone seemed to hate her so much. Sure, she had been kind of a dick at the gate but did she really deserve this kind of treatment? No wonder her dad and aunt didn't want to join them, and just stayed in their own tiny houses.

When Kat had been around seven or eight, her mother had signed her up for the girl scouts. She had walked in ready to meet new friends and make cheesy crafts. She had worn her favorite T-shirt for the occasion and one of the girls made a snide comment about it. And that was it. She spent the rest of the meeting by herself listening to the rest of the girls whisper about the weird girl. There was no redemption to be had, no amends to be made. Her fate had been sealed by an unfortunate clothing choice. She held her tears until her mother came to pick her up but cried the whole way home. Heaven was beginning to feel like that endless Girl Scout meeting.

A thought hit her just then. *I think these fuckers mean to drive people into their houses. I think that is their intention. But is it to keep Heaven for themselves, or is it to keep people from exploring? Heaven seems to hold secrets, like the rip where the demon poked through. Are the angels guarding against that knowledge?* On earth, any rotten or sinful deed could be forgiven. But Kat didn't feel much forgiveness. The greatest commandment was to love God. Maybe she hadn't kissed enough god butt.

Kat walked through her gate and opened her front door. Lucifer picked his head up from the sofa and hopped down to greet her. She picked him up, and he nuzzled against her chin, purring. She carried him into the kitchen and thought maybe something to eat might be nice. Pasta maybe? Carbs really didn't count in Heaven. A plate of steaming fettuccini Alfredo appeared. She paired it with a nice glass of wine and sat down at her little table to eat. Lucifer sat next to her and didn't once beg for food. Instead, he nestled his head against her leg.

As she ate, she thought about her latest encounter with the angels. They sucked for sure. But the longer she sat here and ate what was by far the best plate of pasta she had ever tasted, her anger faded. Sitting here in her perfect little kitchen, the whole ugly mess began to bug her a little less. She looked down at her plate and decided she was done.

She rose from the table and walked to her liquor cabinet. The thought of her father entered her mind, slurring his words with tears standing in his eyes. She didn't remember opening the cabinet door and taking out the bottle, but it was in her hands. She threw it as hard as she could to the floor, where it shattered. Almost as soon as it hit the floor, the mess vanished, and another bottle appeared in its place. In her hand. She set it on the counter this time, where it stayed.

She would not let them drive her into hiding. She would not give in to the tainted pleasures this place offered. *Ooo donut!* She grabbed one and put it in her mouth, letting the sugar dissolve on her tongue. Lucifer was looking up at her from the floor.

"What are you looking at little fucker?" she said through a mouthful of donut.

Kat dropped her robe on the floor of her room. She padded barefoot into the bathroom and drew a bath. She would need to think about this some more. The most important commandment was to love God. Once you did that, he didn't seem to care what you did. Her next door neighbor was proof of that.

No one seemed to mind what happened in their own little cages. But what if someone were to come right out with it? They wanted to drive her into her home, where the donuts were endless and so was the booze.

She remembered her mom, her silly old cat, and the sadness of her aunt and Dad. Heaven's happiness was an illusion. One built on selfishness and indulgence. The memories of her life were already becoming weak. She was afraid she might lose them completely. This place was not feeling like paradise. Was she the one asshole who didn't want to be in Heaven? Kat was done trying to be nice. She was going to have some real fun, and damn anyone who got in her way. Even if it meant damning herself in the process.

Chapter 11

Kat didn't know if one could get kicked out of Heaven, but she wasn't sure she cared anymore. She spent her entire life as an outcast of sorts. Someone who bumble-fucked her way through life. When that hadn't worked, she slashed her way through with a machete. She had never relied on anyone or anything to tell her what to do or how to do it. Really, she had spent her 26 living years pissing people off because she refused to conform. Why stop now that she was dead?

She could feel the pull of the temptation just to stay where she was at. To give up the fight and just let Heaven have its way. Heaven, God, Jesus or whoever, was pushing her to let go. To drown in the pleasures, they granted her. She would not let Heaven erase who she was. She would not let these asses bully her into hiding.

Kat would put it all out in front of their noses. She hoped if she made enough noise, they might leave her alone or maybe help find her damned cat. Anything to shut her up. It wasn't like she could make herself less popular than she already was.

Lucifer wandered into the bathroom as she lay in the tub

full of bubbles. He looked up at her, and she wanted to resent him. He was a symbol of the lie of Heaven. He meowed, and she melted. He might not be an actual cat in the earth sense, but he was real enough to her here. She reached down and patted his head with her wet hand. He didn't mind.

"You sure are fucking weird," she said to him, as he stared at her.

The angels wanted her to hide. Like any other bullies, they wanted to feel superior to others. She needed to show them she wasn't ashamed of herself. No one, angel or otherwise, would bully her into submission.

Kat stepped out of the tub. She walked out of the bathroom and into her bedroom. By the time she got to her enormous bed, she was dry. She laid down naked and stared at the ceiling. She thought of the angels. The wretched, awful stuck-up angels with their smug faces and stupid halos. Their glittering wings. *Wings.* She could get some wings and fly. She had yet to see one angel use their wings to fly. She wondered if they allowed flight at all. That would be pretty cool. Maybe all she needed to do was praise God. Well then, she would praise the fuck out of him.

Kat rolled off her bed and walked through her carpeted bedroom and into her closet. She stared at her naked self in the mirror. Surprised once again at her own flawless body. It disturbed more than just about everything else in Heaven. She willed her scars to return. They refused. That her body was so perfect was the ultimate show of the deception of the place. Her face was flawless as well. She tried to wish a zit into existence, but to no avail.

Kat assumed the position, got down on her knees and drew her hands together in prayer. But stood up again when she decided she probably shouldn't be naked when she praised God. She grabbed a robe from her closet, a gold one, and pulled it over her head.

Kat got back down on her knees. She bowed her head, closed her eyes and said, "Oh God who art in… well here. How I love thee. I am so grateful to be here, you are the one and only creator." She lifted her head slightly to look up and opened one eye. When she got nothing, she continued, "God you are so awesome, the best creator ever." Still nothing so she added, "So much better than that dickhead Satan."

A tingle crept up from the small of her back to in between her shoulder blades. She turned a little in the mirror. Two small sparkling wings had appeared. So far, so good. She tried to wiggle the wings, and they responded in kind. She tried to flap them, and they obeyed. Feeling a strange pull of the muscles in her back and her feet floated up off the carpet.

Holy shitballs! I can fly! She drifted back to the floor.

Not sure if flying was something she would need to practice, she floated up off the floor by flapping her wings. It came naturally. She was glad. She wouldn't want to be wobbly in the skies of Heaven. It would be hard to look cool if she were to lumber around Heaven like a kid trying to learn to ice skate. Suddenly she remembered that she could change her make-up and she wished for the perfect smoky eye. It clashed spectacularly with her ethereal golden robe. A whore in angels clothing.

Kat walked out of her bedroom, Lucifer had been watching from her bed, fascinated. She went through her living room but paused at the front door. She wondered if she was making a huge mistake. Was she about to damn herself to Hell? Maybe sit in limbo? Her mouth went dry. She took a wobbly step away from her door and into her kitchen. She wanted a drink of water and one appeared. She collected her thoughts as she sipped. She hadn't been thirsty, but the water satisfied her just the same. She closed her eyes for a moment. When she opened them, they fell upon the pink box on the table. *Ooo donut!*

Kat reached for a donut but stopped herself. No. That's what they want. She steadied herself on her weakened knees and walked to the front door. She took what she wished was a deep breath and opened it revealing the beautiful sunshine in Heaven.

Karen was outside in her yard enjoying the sunshine too. When she saw Kat, she sneered at her over her glass of wine. Kat noticed her wine glass had the words 'Live, Laugh, Love' etched onto it like the picture above her sofa. *Sure live, laugh, love, murder your family, whatevs.* Kat blew a kiss at her, before lifting off her feet and into the blue sky. Karen smiled a knowing smile as she lifted off. Had Kat seen it, she might have wondered why.

She stayed low to the ground. She figured she could not be injured but being up in the air still made her uneasy. Kat fluttered her wings, learning how they worked. She flew up and the breeze tickled her body in the loveliest way. She rose above the tree in her yard. Aware of Karen's disapproving eyes on her. Jeffrey was still in his awful little house. From this vantage point, the landscape was breathtaking. Or would have been had she had any breath to take.

She could see for miles, and she wondered if she might find the waterfall where Aunt Judy had found her little wolf demon with the excellent pot. Seemed a good thing to remember. She had to wonder why no one else had thought to fly like this. Flying people should fill the sky, doing loop de loops and prancing through the clouds. But she was the only one. The sky was an empty expanse of the purest blue, dotted with patches of white clouds. The sun was warm on her robe, and a feeling of utter peace filled her. *There's a catch here I bet.* She figured she might as well enjoy it before she found out what it was. She was currently in the fuck around part, the finding out would probably suck balls.

She soared above the rooftops and trees. From here, she had one hell of a view. Heaven was endless it seemed. Which would make sense. There must be billions and billions of inhabitants. Heaven would get crowded if it were limited by the constraints of limited land mass. It would never run out of room. That would make it impossible to see it all. She could fly forever and never run out of room, or so it seemed.

She faltered in the air then and then slipped lower in the sky. If Heaven had no boundaries that would mean that she would never be able to leave. A sudden sense of anxiety overcame her. Kat hated nothing more than the thought of being restricted. Up here in the air, gazing down at Heaven made her feel trapped. *Well, now you're just being silly. Who the fuck worries about being trapped in Heaven?* The thought retreated into a deep recess in her mind, where it went to sleep, but did not die.

Kat was in search of the angels now. She flew over the angel bar, but it was empty. She flew over the houses and the Administration building, but still nothing. *Where the fuck are they?* She flew over the spot where she had seen Jesus talking before. One or two of the awful creatures were standing around, talking shit no doubt. The platform was empty.

She glided right over the top of them, ruffling Lyla's golden hair. The pale angel didn't even flinch. Just smoothed her hair back in place and kept talking to the other angel standing next to her, a dark-haired male who seemed to be just as unperturbed.

Kat would not have any of this. She flew closer this time but with the same result. She touched down on the platform. The sole of her foot touched down unevenly, so instead of the graceful landing she had intended, she tilted sideways and lost her balance. She fell right off the small stage and into the dirt.

"Hey there Kathy," Lyla said, with a horrific gleam in her

eye. The two angels burst out laughing.

Kat still lay in the dirt not hurt but stunned just the same. What was it about the angels that left her completely without any stinging comebacks? It's like their Heaven granted them some sort of smart-ass shield. The two angels had turned back to her and were giggling now with each other. She got back up to her feet and tried not to stumble. She made it, but just barely. She smoothed out her hair and brushed the Heaven dirt off of herself. The angels had lost interest completely.

Since she seemed to have nothing clever to say, she opted to say nothing at all. She lifted off again, leaving the angels to snicker. She soared into the air much faster than she had intended and the sky went blurry. She tried to slow down, but her wings were unresponsive. She was hurtling toward she had no idea what, like a huge glittering hummingbird. Air was rushing past her, and her robe flapped. While she was still immune to the shivers, the sensation was unpleasant. Kat started to panic.

She had lost any control over her wings and herself. She was powerless to stop herself from propelling upward. She closed her eyes and let it happen. She really didn't have a choice in the matter. At least she wouldn't die, again. But that thought did little to quell the fear she had.

Then all at once, it stopped. She slammed into her yard, landing next to the swing in her front yard. She lay there, unhurt but rattled. When she turned her head, she was eye level with the grass. She sat up and saw that she had left an indent in the ground in the shape of her body. *Well, what do you know? I made a dirt angel,* and a little giggle escaped her.

"I guess you figured out that you can't control Heaven's wings. God's awesome power is not to be fooled with. Didn't you notice that no one else was flying? Dumb slut," Karen yelled to her from her yard.

"Don't you have some kids to murder or something?" Kat asked, and as she got up her legs were still wobbly. She fell right back in the hole she had made.

Jeffrey Dahmer was watching the whole affair with a face made of stone. She wondered what he was thinking and then decided she didn't want to know.

Kat stood up. When she turned to look at the hole she had made, her sparkly wings lay embedded in the dirt. Good fucking riddance. Karen was still smirking at her from her yard as she watched Kat retreat into her house.

Chapter 12

Lucifer was at the door as she walked through hanging her head. He followed her as she flopped down on the couch. It sucked her in like quicksand, but without all the death and suffocation. She became aware of the goofy gold robe clinging to her and began to pull at it aggressively. It stretched and pulled, but the more she pulled at it, the more entangled she became. She just wanted to be free of the ridiculous thing, and then she was. Which only made her feel more stupid. Lucifer watched the whole affair with love in his eyes.

She collapsed back onto the sofa, and Lucifer crawled onto her lap. He snuggled his head under her chin, snuck his rough tongue out of his mouth and licked her face.

"Eeew," Kat said, before she remembered he had not been licking his butthole.

Lucifer snuggled up to her and she stroked his soft fur. He began to purr. She allowed him to comfort her and was grateful for his company. She thought about going back to her dad's place to see if he could offer any advice, but the last time had made her feel even worse. He had been placating himself with booze and would likely just tell her to do the same. She wished she knew how to help him, but he didn't seem like he would accept it even if she could.

Aunt Judy was much the same. She had not been open to anything other than hanging out with her cats and her bong. The thought of any dissent had scared her to the point of getting angry. She really wanted to find the demon, but she had no idea of how without Judy's help. And Judy had made it clear that she would not help her.

Kat felt isolated. Her thoughts turned to her mother, whose face was becoming unclear. Was she terrified that her daughter was roasting in Hell? She had wondered when she first got here how anyone could be happy here knowing their loved one might be in pain on earth, but now she knew. Heaven simply erased their memories. You can't worry about it if you don't remember what you are supposed to be worried about. The glimmer of her mother was still there, though. She concentrated on her mother's face. She pictured her tucking her in, wiping the sweat off her forehead when she had the flu. The face in her memories became clearer.

In her mind, she saw her mother sitting in a pew in a church she didn't recognize. Her mother was the same age as she had been when Kat slammed into the tree. This didn't seem like a memory. Her mother was holding her rosary and sobbing. *This is now.* Kat's heart ached to contact her. Just to let her know she was cool and in Heaven. Kat concentrated as hard as she could. With her eyes closed, she tried to reach her mother.

She reached out to touch her. A few strands of the gray hair that littered the top of her head stirred. She tried even harder, she could see her fingers reaching, coming close, but not quite making contact. Her mother stirred. She was so close.

"Mom!" Kat said, but her mother could not hear her. She tried again but got nothing.

Kat felt weak, her concentration was fading. She was losing the connection, but she tried hard to keep it. She was so close. She couldn't give up. She gave one last spectral push, before being rudely yanked into her own space. Connection lost. When she tried to concentrate again, she felt drained. Used up. Her eyes filled with tears, but they did not fall. Lucifer crawled up and licked her cheek again. Kat brushed him away, but gently.

She pulled herself up, and out of her couch and into her bedroom. She pulled on a white robe. She went back out to the living room and past the kitchen to the front door. She caught the pink box out of the corner of her eye. *Ooo donut!* She grabbed one as she walked out the door and stuffed it in her mouth with exactly no joy whatsoever.

She kept her focus as she walked to the Administration building. Determined not to get lost in her thoughts. She would complete this task and then be as complacent as they wanted. She would not rest until she could reach her mother.

She bounded up the steps and pulled open the door. The angel behind the counter watched her as she almost ran up to meet him.

"I see you found the perfect smoky eye, Kathy," he said.

She had forgotten to change her make-up.

"Please let me talk to my mom. I saw her. I was almost there. I just need a little help to let her know I'm cool. Then I'll stop bugging. I'll behave. Whatever you want. I can't rest until I know she is ok, please," She hung on the last word.

The angel looked at her for much too long, before looking down at the counter. He seemed to consider something. When he looked up again, he had a nasty gleam in his eye. She hated him, but he was still hot as fuck.

"Sorry, that is God's will. You can't change that. Give it some time, Kathy. You will be at peace," he said.

"Yeah, I know I'm supposed to forget. I won't though. It is so rotten to leave her hurting like that. There must be something I can do."

"God works in mysterious ways, Kathy. We are not to question His plan; we are only to trust and love Him. Maybe it was you that caused her pain and made her afraid for your soul?" he said again, maintaining the creepy eye contact. "You can always talk to Jesus, Kathy," he said, his smile had become malicious.

"I don't want to talk to that self-absorbed asshat!" She spit at the angel. *Why did this fucker keep calling her Kathy? And why despite being an utter dick head was he so fucking cute?*

"All will become clear in time, Kathy," he said, his halo glowed just a little brighter. He was enjoying this.

"You know what? Fuck you. And where the fuck is my damned cat?" She turned away and started toward the door. "Oh yeah, stop calling me Kathy!" Her screams echoed off the walls.

She pushed open the huge door. Immediately, she was hit in the face with heavenly sunlight. She turned to slam the door, but even with all the effort she could muster, it closed with a soft swoosh. She kicked it and was stunned to see her bare big toe bend the wrong direction. *Huh, I guess I can still be surprised.* There was no pain, and her toe bent right back into place.

She passed a snickering gaggle of angels as she stomped back to her house. Lyla stood in the middle of them. It was like they knew her plight. Kat had to wonder if the halos came with some sort of telepathy. Or it could be that St. Peter had simply tipped them off and put a target on her back? It was just like the strip club drama on earth.

The first strip club she had worked in had a clique of what she came to know as OG's or Original Gangsters. Dancers that had been around for a while. They ruthlessly mocked and terrorized the new girls. Their circle was almost impossible to break into. Kat had managed for a little while to avoid their wrath, but one unfortunate move brought her to their attention. She had approached a regular customer of one of the head OG's by mistake, and that was the end. She found her make-up case glued to the counter, lotion dumped through the vents in her locker, and a vicious rumor that she had herpes. She could not make amends, and she left and found another club. These angels were Heaven's OG's, except she couldn't just up and leave. She would have to deal with them forever. It was like she was in her own little version of Hell. And maybe that was the joke? A whole ass backwards plan to make her think she was in Heaven, but she was really in Hell. If so, it was brilliant. The only thing that would make it worse would be Nickelback's debut album playing on repeat forever. She quickly snuffed out the thought. She definitely didn't want to make that happen even on accident. So far that was the only thing that made her think she might actually be in Heaven and not Hell. The merciful lack of terrible rock/pop music.

When her little jasmine covered gate came into view, she decided she would rather keep walking. Walking and fuming. Fuming and walking. Who would've thought that Heaven would be so fucked up? And yet she was still convinced that Hell would be worse. All that fire and pain. Lakes of sulfur. Didn't sulfur smell like rotten eggs? An eternity burning was bad enough, but the stench of deviled egg farts forever. No thanks.

Still, Heaven sucked pretty badly. God seemed like a dick, and Jesus was useless. She thought of her never-ending bottle of whiskey. She could sit in a bubble bath getting fucked up forever. And there was the endless supply of donuts. Tempting, but no. Kat did not give up, not even when she was dead.

The sound of water up ahead brought her out of her head and back to the cobblestone lane she was walking on. The trees had grown thicker as she walked and the houses sparser. The sound grew louder as she walked. The houses ended at a lush dense forest. The trees were so thick and some of them so close together she had to squeeze sideways to get through them. The water sounded like it was just on the other side of them, she followed it.

The bush and the trees were so thick that she wasn't sure she could push through them, but she persisted. Her curiosity driving her. She thought she might need a chainsaw and was dismayed that one didn't appear in her hand. Odd.

She pushed through a tangle of branches that should have ripped open her glittery skin but did not. Squeezing and pushing she made it through. The source of the sound now apparent. A massive waterfall was crashing into a crystal blue pool in the middle of the clearing. She followed it upwards to where it was pouring over the edge of a rock cliff. The sun shone through the mist at the top creating a magnificent rainbow. If she had lungs, the sight of it would have been breathtaking.

There was nothing in her mind as she stared up at the waterfall. To one side of it, there was an outcropping of stones. They formed a pile with large smooth ones at the top. She walked over to it and climbed up. She sat to watch the waterfall. On the other side stood several flower patches with blossoms on it that she was sure she had never seen before. She waited to see the squirrels and birds hopping around in them, but none did. She looked up to the nearest trees and noticed that there were no animals there either. Weird. This was the first place where she had seen no animals at all. They were all around, part of the landscape, frolicking to and fro. They were everywhere but here.

Something was off about this place. Like she shouldn't be there. It was Heaven. She should be able to go anywhere she wanted. But the incident with the wings proved that to be an illusion. The illusion of freedom was strong but became weak and permeable if you pushed the boundaries. Heaven wanted you to think you could do whatever you wanted, but if you went beyond where they wanted you to, they would pull you back. Heaven was just a beautiful lie where the truth was hidden and meant to stay that way. She shuddered, and for the first time, a hint of a shiver moved through her. Cold but not quite. She had the distinct feeling that she should go back to her house.

"Pssst" a voice whispered from just below her butt. "You want some drugs?"

Chapter 13

Amon.
A hot flame licked up from under the stone she was sitting on.

"Sorry," the demon said. "I puke flames sometimes."

Aunt Judy seemed afraid of Amon when she had spoken about him, but it was kind of hard not to be afraid of a demon from Hell. Still, Kat tried to keep an open mind. At the very least, she should end up with some good pot.

"Uh, it's ok. Are you alright? Can I get you some water maybe?" Kat was trying to be hospitable.

"No, that won't help. It only happens when I come through the portal to Heaven. In Hell, all is gravy. No flaming barfs. At least not for me," he said.

There was the sound of shuffling under her, and she moved off the stone to see if she could get a look at her new friend. She hoped he would be her friend. So far, making friends in Heaven hadn't been going well. Kat didn't want to find out what would happen if she pissed off this one. The angels hated her, and she didn't need a demon on her case as well.

Kat must have missed the dark space between the stones

when she climbed up to sit. A puff of smoke oozed out of the dark spot, followed by a face that resembled a dog of sorts. No. A wolf. All Kat saw was a snout and eyes. Smoke drifted from between its jaws. She tried to conceal her alarm at his appearance. She forced a cordial smile to her lips.

"I'm Kat. I think my aunt told me about you," she said.

"I'm Amon. Judy, right? Hot chick who wears an ugly orange robe? Likes the ganja?" He said.

"That would be Aunt Judy. She said you like that orange fruit," Kat replied, feeling a little more at ease. Amon seemed nice, albeit a little hard to look at.

"That stuff is amazing. I can't get it in Hell. Technically, I'm not supposed to be here, but I can't get enough of that stuff. And as long as I don't come all the way through the portal, it's all good. But it gives me terrible heartburn. Not the fruit, Heaven." Amon laughed, before hiccupping and expelling a large burst of fire.

The flame touched Kat's hair and set it alight. She yelped and patted her head, extinguishing the flames. Her scorched hair grew back in an instant.

"Sorry," Amon said, giving her a sheepish look from under his furry brow. He was almost cute. Almost.

"It's ok. I don't think you can hurt me," she said.

"I can if I want," his eyes narrowed, and he produced a low growl.

Kat backed away but stopped when Amon burst out laughing.

"Just kidding. I can't hurt you. I wouldn't want to either. I'm a demon, not an asshole," he said. "Now get me some of that fruit!"

His eyes glowed red and he retched as flames erupted from his mouth, pouring past his sharp teeth. Kat backed away for real this time, preparing to run.

"Ha! Scared you good that time! For real though, can you get me some? I got whatever you want. As long as it's weed." Amon's face went back to normal, and he wore a big goofy grin.

"Yeah, but you can't ever do that again. Not funny," Kat was shaking.

She looked around and saw a tree that bore the fruit he was looking for. She lifted her robe, exposing her smooth, hairless lump. She gathered about half a dozen of the plump ripe orange colored fruit in it. She brought it back to the pile of stones where Amon was waiting, the goofy grin still on his face. She stayed a few feet away. They hadn't finished negotiating.

"Well, that's a nice Barbie doll pussy you got there," he said with a smile full of razor blades.

"Thanks." Kat frowned and rolled her eyes. "How about some weed, and something to smoke it with?"

Amon disappeared into the crack and reappeared a moment later with a pretty green glass pipe, a lighter, and a big bag of weed. He did not emerge from the space, nor did he hold the items out of it.

"Give me the fruit first. Sorry, but lots of shitheads in Heaven. The first time I tried this, some asshole burned me. Took my shit and tried to get me to chase him. I nearly puked lava. I got to know I can trust you," he said.

His look had darkened a little, but she figured he was right to be leery. She had met some real shitheads here too. She handed the fruit over without making a move to for the weed. He took it and handed her the goods. She smiled at him. This demon seemed alright. But then again, so had Karen. And Karen was pretty fucking far from alright.

"Go on, try it. It's some pretty good shit," he said, opening his jaws and taking a monster bite of the fruit. "I can't take this stuff down there. Shit gets funky as it goes through the portal, it will rot before I get it back to Hell."

"That makes sense, I guess." She wasn't really sure what made sense anymore.

She opened the bag and packed the bowl of her pipe. The demon watched her and took another bite of his fruit, pure bliss in his eyes. She lit it and drew in. It was heavenly, or hell-y maybe, either way Kat was delighted as her head fogged over and her eyelids drooped.

"So, tell me about Hell," she said as the smoke billowed out of her mouth.

Amon looked amused as he started on his second piece of fruit.

"Well, it's better than this place for sure. For one thing, murderers get their due. If you're a shithead, you get what's coming to you. Lots of people came to Hell because they didn't repent. Or were just non-believers. Plenty of good atheists that got sent to Hell. We got Stephen Hawking, Mark Twain, and tons of others. We have some lively parties," he said. The fur around his mouth was dripping with juice and bits of fruit flesh.

"What about the lakes of hell fire and torture and stuff? There isn't anything like that here as far as I can tell, but Heaven hasn't been much like the paradise stuff I was led to believe. I mean the amenities are great and there's no pain, and holy shit the food, but the people kind of suck. I've started to wonder if this place might be Hell after all. How stupid is that?" Kat asked.

"You're definitely in Heaven, but really Heaven and Hell are just human concepts. I'd feel like I was in Hell if I had to be where you are. It's all pretty subjective and relative. Well, we do have lakes of fire and stuff, but only in some places. The weather is not all that bad. It even rains sometimes. No one gets tortured who doesn't earn it. Stalin has it pretty bad, but really, who cares? Cause fuck that guy. Mostly we sit around and shoot the shit. The food is pretty great. Sex is even better. The music is fabulous. There is pain, but you will heal if you are careful. Not any more than is on earth. Most people are friendly in Hell. And we have all the animals," he said. "Well, almost all of them. Some dogs go to Hell, but just the ones that shit on the floor. Just kidding. I'm actually not sure why we get some and not all the dogs."

Kat dropped her pipe as her jaw fell open, and it shattered on the rocks.

"Animals go to Hell? Is my cat there? He's going to be so mad," Kat said.

"Yeah, but they're well cared for, man. Animals are innocent, and you can earn Hell's punishment by hurting any of them. Your cat is probably in Hell, but he's cool, I'm sure. He's a cat though, so he's definitely pissed at you." Amon said. He turned and reached into the space and brought out another pipe and held it out to her. "Here. Ya dummy."

"What about contacting the living?"

"That can be a little tricky. It's rare, but they will let it happen sometimes," he said. "Are you thinking about trying to get to Hell?"

"You know, I might be. The angels are real dicks. My dad won't stay sober. Aunt Judy is cool, but she got mad at me for asking to find you. She is really afraid of Hell, and honestly, I think she might be afraid of God too. Jesus is a real fucking weirdo. And I miss my cat. I have one here, but he's kind of weird too. I got an endless box of donuts and booze. Do you think I could get into Hell if I wanted to?" Kat was rambling.

Amon took a bite of his last piece of fruit and chewed thoughtfully.

"Well, Satan was thrown out of Heaven, but I can't think of anyone else. I suppose it's possible, but I would think you probably couldn't just ask for a transfer. God is pretty possessive of his souls. He doesn't ever let them go. Part of his beef with Satan I guess. I don't know of anyone who has left Heaven," he said. "I guess you could try to get thrown out? You'd have to be a real pain in the ass."

She thought she had used up all of her fucks about staying in Heaven, but now as she was seriously considering going to Hell, she thought she might still have a couple fucks left. She liked warm weather but spending an eternity in Hell?

"Can you ask Satan to bring me down?" Kat asked hopefully.

"No. Satan wouldn't do that. You'll have to get there on your own. I'm not even sure I could bring you through this portal. I tried that with a piece of fruit, and it rotted and disintegrated. Who knows what would happen to your soul? I think you should keep trying. I have a feeling you could really piss people off," Amon said with a grotesque wink.

"You're not wrong there. I got into a bit of a spat with St. Peter at the gates, when I thought I was going to Hell anyway. I think he made it hard for me in here. He told everyone I was a huge slut. I mean he wasn't wrong, but still. I gave him the finger too," she said and it was her turn to give a sheepish look.

"Well, you're probably on your way already! And we love sluts in Hell!" Amon gave her another wink, and Kat cringed. It did nothing to improve his looks.

Amon wiped his face with the back of his hand and let out a huge flaming burp. Kat didn't flinch this time when the fire warmed her face and singed her eyebrows. They came back perfect. She didn't even bother to check.

"Man, it was nice meeting you, Kat. I got to go. Come back when you run out of weed. If you toss a pebble into this hole, I'll know you're there. Good luck with your damnation! And tell your aunt I said Hey," he said before disappearing down the hole.

How sweet of him to wish her damned, but she didn't

think she would mention him to Aunt Judy. She hopped off her stone and onto the ground. Her head was spinning. As she walked out of the forest, she stopped to pluck a piece of fruit from the tree. Heaven munchies. She took a bite and understood why the demon was so fond of it. The juice streamed off of her face in thick rivulets.

Buster was in Hell. No wonder they were being so elusive. What would they say? Your cat is in Hell, but don't worry he's having a great time? Everything she learned about Heaven and Hell during her life seemed to be turned on its head. She thought about what Aunt Judy had said about not trusting the demon. She had a point. Should she really trust a drug-dealing demon from Hell?

Her head was clearing as she walked. The sun was going down, and she was thinking a little bit of sleep might do her some good. Reset her brain. That bed was awfully comfortable, and it would feel nice to lie down and close her eyes. The more she thought about it, the more she thought Aunt Judy might be right. What was she thinking? To let a demon talk her into getting sent to Hell. Of course, he would say it was better down there. He's a fucking demon.

Something sparkled in the road ahead of her, right before her little gate. Her vision was still a little fuzzy from the pot. She squinted, and the something came into focus. Lyla. The angel was standing right outside her gate.

"Hey Kathy, the whore. Your little stunt today was pretty stupid. I just wanted to tell you, you had better stay in your little house. If I see you again, you'll be sorry," the angel said.

Kat just stared at her, thinking if she wasn't stoned, she might have something cool to say. But no. She tried anyway.

"Stupid angel, no one likes you either," Kat stammered as she pushed past the winged creature and into her yard. *Fuck me. That was a stupid thing to say,* she thought as she opened the door to her house.

The angel took flight and gracefully flew away. Lucifer

hopped off the couch to meet her and she picked him up. He nuzzled her face.

"That's it, little buddy, this place sucks ass and I don't think I'm going to stay." Lucifer licked her face.

Chapter 14

Kat awoke in her bed after a good long sleep. The events of the day before fresh and clear in her mind. She had met the demon, and he was pretty cool. She had just about talked herself out of trusting the furry little dude when the angel convinced her that while Amon might be ugly, the angels in Heaven were far uglier.

She was going to get kicked out of Heaven. Well, she was going to try anyway. You'd think it wouldn't be that hard, but yesterday's antics had seemed to prove otherwise. She didn't make the commotion she thought she was going to. But then again, she had upset the pale angel enough to come to her home. That had to be something. She remembered the graceful way the angel had flown off, so unlike her own bumbling attempt. She wasn't going to bother with the wings anymore. She had learned that lesson the hard way.

So, what next? She thought of the hunky angel at the Administration building. He was so maddening and yet so handsome. What was his name again? Oh, who cares? Could she corrupt him? Kat decided she was going to find out. Come hell or high water, she was going to try.

A wanton display of lust should gain her some ground.

The deliberate defiling of God's angel should be enough to get her thrown out. But how do you tempt an angel? Especially one that had no dick? On earth, she had been a professional temptress, had she not repented she would not be in this predicament? The irony of it all was a bit much.

On her nightstand was the bag of weed and pipe. She filled up the pipe, brought it to her lips, lit it, and drew in a large quantity of smoke. She blew it out in perfect little rings. She tried to blow them into different shapes. A perfect little smoke star left her lips and floated to the ceiling. Neat. She lay there, smoked, and pondered how to best tempt an angel. Tempting earthly men had been an almost mindless task. Get naked, shake your butt a little and voila! You've made your rent in 15 minutes. Angels would not be that easy.

So, what do angels want? She should start there; they must desire something. She presumed they started out as human, so there might be a glimmer of sexual desire remaining beneath their shimmering skin and 'Holier than thou' attitudes. No penis, no erection, no drive. Sex was probably not going to happen. But then again, she had had some glimmer of an orgasm when she really tried. Like a missing limb that still gets phantom feelings.

What if she were to take the halo. Not steal it, but just borrow it for a minute. Set it aside like taking off a piece of jewelry. At the very least, it would piss him off. Assuming she could get it off at all. She took another hit from her pipe. Lucifer had become aware that she was awake and had snuggled up against her, purring. Kat thought she might be on to something. She had no idea what would happen. But fuck it. She had nothing to lose.

The munchies were starting to kick in and pancakes came to mind. And then they were on a tray on her lap. Breakfast in bed? Don't mind if I do. She dug into the plate of steaming blueberry-covered pancakes with all the gusto of a proper stoner. A cup of coffee would go nicely with these. And a large mug of the stuff appeared. She took a long drink and began to feel the caffeine start to counter the effects of the pot. A lovely combination.

When she had enough, she just had the thought, and they were gone. She flipped back the covers and hopped out of bed. She walked to her closet and pulled on a robe. This one a soft purple. She hated it.

She left her closet to find Lucifer staring at her, which was pretty much his primary function.

"Well? What do you think little fuzzy dude?" Kat asked, as if she was trying on a new outfit and not the same fucking thing in a different color.

Lucifer responded with an approving meow.

"You know, I kind of wish you could talk," she said.

"Ok," Lucifer answered. "You look gorgeous."

Kat was impressed, although she would have been more so had she not been in Heaven.

"Thank you, little buddy," she said smiling at the creature. "Is my hair good, maybe I should change it up a little?"

"Hmmm. How about a little curlier? Maybe just a darker shade? Some highlights?" he suggested.

Kat padded to the bathroom to look in the mirror. She went with a few more waves and added a few light streaks. She turned to her talking Heaven cat.

"Well?" She said.

"Perfect. What about make-up? Maybe a little darker? Longer lashes?" He said.

He was quite the fashion aficionado, although she suspected he was just voicing her own thoughts. She didn't mind though. It felt less awkward than talking to herself, but still a little nutty. She did as he suggested and looked ready to fuck with an angel.

"Thanks, dude," she smiled at him and picked him up. He licked her face.

Kat walked through her living room and to her front door. Lucifer followed her into the living room to take his spot on the couch.

"Good luck, I'll be awaiting your return," Lucifer said.

She gave him a wave before she walked out the door. The sun was shining because of course it was. Jeffrey was standing outside his door, looking like a serial killer. There was something brownish red smeared on his face and a gruesome smile appeared on his lips as she caught his attention. She frowned at him but didn't wave. Karen's yard was blessedly empty.

She remembered the annoying neighbor she had at her apartment when she was alive. She had been an evangelical Christian who liked to leave religious tracts on Kat's door and then pretend she did not know how it got there. Betty her name had been, at least Kat was fairly sure it had been Betty. She wondered what Betty would think about spending an eternity with shitty angels and serial killer neighbors. She had thought living next to a stripper was bad; just wait until the poor thing got to Heaven.

Kat stepped out of her gate and on to the cobblestone road. The scent of jasmine was almost overwhelming, cloying. She had loved it at first, but Heaven seemed to lose a little of its luster as she pursued her dream of going to Hell. There were birds flying and just a hint of wispy clouds in the sky. She started on her way. Some of the other inhabitants of Heaven were in their yards and some waved to her as she passed. Not one of them made any attempt at conversation. At first, she had thought that it was rude, but now she knew they were wallowing in their own customized pleasures in Heaven. They were content in their tiny houses. Happy with whatever bliss lay within. Jeffery's bloodstained smiling face appeared in her mind, and she winced.

The shining Administration building was just ahead, and Kat kind of wished it had been farther. She was enjoying her barefooted walk in the sun, but she reminded herself that Heaven wanted her to be distracted from her task. Not unlike what she had done for her customers at the strip club. Distraction was the point. She had worked to take their minds off of their troubles. She would not be Heaven's hapless strip club customer. Not today, Heaven, not today.

She hopped up the steps but paused at the door. She had come here intending to start some shit with an angel but had given very little thought about the execution of the act. *Could it be the weed?* She had only gotten as far as to think she was going to see if she could snag his halo, as to what would come after she really hadn't thought about it. As she stood with her hand on the handle, she thought about how to do that. Should she just reach up and take it? Maybe she could just knock it off his head. Could she even reach the thing at her height? She didn't even know if it could be removed.

She reached a hand up and touched the golden ring floating above her head. It didn't feel like it was attached to anything. She tried to pull it and it felt like it was caught on something. She yanked really hard, and the thing came loose with an audible rip. The force of her pulling knocked her off balance and she tumbled down the stone steps. Her halo slipped out of her hands, hit the ground, and bounced away. She braced herself and tried to stand, but her leg was bent the wrong way causing her to fall back onto her ass. And then came the pain.

She felt every torn muscle and broken bone. She looked around to see if anyone had seen, but she was alone. She looked around for her halo. It had rolled under a small shrub, and she crawled carefully over to retrieve it. A strange but familiar sensation trickled down from her stomach and between her thighs. She touched herself through her robe and was astounded to find her pussy had returned. With a vengeance.

Glancing around to make sure no one was looking, and when she was sure there wasn't she lifted her robe. It was back. In all it its glory. In spite of her pain, she felt she must explore. She ran a little circle around the little man in the boat and the orgasm hit her almost instantly. It knocked her off her feet again and she fell back down to the ground panting. *Holy fuckballs!* She picked up her halo and reluctantly put it back on her head. Her pussy disappeared again, but her leg healed instantly. Armed with what she suspected was a heavenly secret, she stood up and walked back up the stairs to the Administration building. She didn't hesitate to open the door this time.

She was dismayed to see there was a line at the counter waiting to talk to the angel. Butterflies took up residence in her stomach once again, as she took her place at the end of the line. There were three people ahead of her. She thought about turning and leaving, maybe to come back later. The man at the counter was thanking the angel and walking away toward the hallway to Jesus' office. She pitied him. Just two people now, she would wait.

Kat rocked back and forth on her heels anxiously. One more person peeled off from the counter, a woman, this time to the other side of it and into a different hallway. Kat wondered what was down that one. God maybe, saints even. She decided she didn't care much. Just one more person to go, another man. He appeared to be begging for something, but she couldn't hear what he was saying. The angel handed him a slip of paper with a wry smile. The man turned to leave and faced her.

"Careful, that guy is kind of an ass," he said as he

made his way out the door.

Kat shrugged her shoulders in acknowledgement, she knew.

Alone with the angel, she stepped up to the counter. Now that she was looking up at him, she was unsure if she would be able to reach his halo. He was wearing a nametag she must have missed that said "Chad". Figures. She didn't want to think about it too long and lose her nerve. She bent her knees and sprung upward. He flinched in surprise, but not enough to be out of her reach. Bracing herself on the counter she grasped the halo and snatched it off of his head. His eyes widened.

She landed on the floor with a thud with his halo in hand. With the other hand, she grasped her own and yanked. The angel behind the counter did not look pleased, he looked angry. It made him even hotter. He lunged over the counter but stopped short of grabbing her. He towered over her. His look of intense anger startled her. Kat stepped back a step or two, still holding both halos and unsure how to proceed. She had come this far, and she saw no reason to puss out now. She lifted her head up and planted a wet kiss right on his mouth.

The angel softened a little and she thought he was about to kiss her back, and he did for just a moment. Using his mouth as a distraction, he reached around and grabbed his halo out of Kat's hand. As he did, he leaned toward her, and she felt something firm push up against her belly. Before he could replace his halo on his head, she slapped it out of his hand.

He scowled at her. Other people, a mix of angels and regular people had seeped in from the hallways and were watching the spectacle. Kat had given this dude a boner and gained an audience. Showtime. She pulled her robe up to her neck exposing her body. She glanced at the angel whose bulge had gotten bigger despite the halo on his head.

"You got something for me, big boy?" Kat asked. She

licked her lips like a porn star. "Come and get it."

Chad the angel looked perplexed but tempted. He looked around at the other people watching and then back at her. Kat moved toward him and thought he would retreat, but he stood fast. He then moved so quick on her she found herself paralyzed. He had her up off the floor and in his arms. His robe had disappeared. From her vantage point, she couldn't see his chiseled abs and muscled arms. She wouldn't have had time to appreciate it, anyway. He drove himself into her with such force she screamed. Her audience gasped and then grew silent, as the angel did what angels were not supposed to do.

Kat threw her head back as an unearthly orgasm overtook her, and then she found herself on the floor, panting and naked. Chad had recovered his robes, halo, and composure and was staring down at her. She really wished he would learn to back off the intense eye contact thing. It really weirded her out. His robe hung flat along the front of him. He looked as if he wanted to spit at her. Instead, he walked around and took his place at the counter.

She heard a lone clap and turned to see the man who had gone down the hallway to Jesus, smiling and slow clapping in her direction. Sporting his own bulge, he was holding his own halo in his hand. *Good for you dude. Maybe we can hook up later.* She stood up and curtsied back at him. The rest of the crowd looked disgusted. Perfect. She curtsied to them too, and then flipped them all off.

She pulled her robe down over her boobs and set her halo on top of her head before walking unsteadily through the big doors. She wallowed in her sweet revenge. She had just successfully defiled an angel. She wondered if the poor guy would be able to look her in the eyes after that. She thought he probably would. If only because that seemed to be his thing. Her vindication, as far as he was concerned, was complete.

Clouds had gathered and thickened in the sky as she did her deed. The smell of imminent rain filled the air. A low rumble of thunder growled in the sky as she walked back to her place. She could hardly wait to tell Lucifer. He would be proud of her. Maybe not proud, but happy for her at least. Her foot went sideways on the cobblestone, and she almost lost her balance.

A loud crack of lightning flashed in the sky, followed by a crash of thunder. A warm and heavy rain began to fall as she walked. She thought about an umbrella, and one appeared in her hand. She threw it to the ground and let the rain soak her all the way through. Her make-up ran down her face and she smiled all the way home.

Chapter 15

Both of Kat's neighbors appeared to be in their own houses as she stepped through her own gate. For that, she was grateful. As she walked through her door, she peeled off her robe. She was dry by the time Lucifer picked his head up off the sofa to greet her.

"So?" he asked.

"Well, I got the angel to fuck me, short and sweet. I'm not sure if it was enough to get me sent to Hell though. I mean I'm still here, but some other people saw what happens when you take off your halo," she replied.

Kat sat naked on her sofa and stroked Lucifer's head. He began to purr, which made his next words sound as if he had a mouthful of stones.

"You are still here, maybe someone will come get you or something?" he said, pushing his head into her hand to prevent her from stopping petting him.

"I don't have any idea, but I'm thinking that maybe it didn't go far enough. The demon said that he hadn't heard of anyone since Satan getting sent to from Heaven. I think I might have to keep trying," Kat pondered this last thought.

Defiling the angel had been fun for sure, but other than

the thunder and lightning, nothing changed. No dramatic drop through the clouds and earth and into a lake of fire. No booming voice of God, damning her to Hell. Nothing at all. As satisfying as the encounter had been, she was feeling disappointed. Again.

She got up off the sofa and padded into the kitchen as she thought about what to do next. The sun was shining through the window now that the storm had passed. She spotted Karen out in her yard. Karen saw her looking at her and flipped her off. *Yeah, fuck you too,* she thought. Who knew what kept that woman occupied in her house? She thought of her other neighbor and thought maybe she didn't want to know. Looking at Karen standing in her yard full of petunias, Kat was more determined than ever to get the fuck out of Heaven.

They couldn't ignore her forever. If she stayed focused, she would eventually get what she wanted. Her eyes turned to her kitchen table. *Ooo donut!* She picked a pink one with sprinkles out of the box and stuffed it in her mouth as Lucifer sauntered into the kitchen.

"See, they want to ply me with donuts and cats with no assholes," she said, spraying crumbs all over the floor. They disappeared as she looked down. No need to clean in Heaven.

"I'm glad I bring you as much pleasure as the donuts," he said, seeming to be pleased with himself.

Kat swallowed the lump of dough in her mouth and picked up the glass of ice-cold milk that had appeared next to the box. She hadn't really even thought of it. Heaven was getting predictive. Like a creepy autocorrect. Just another reason to get out of here. But she was still a little afraid of Hell. She knew the demon might be lying. But he had seemed like the only genuine thing she had met here. If what he said was true, then Hell was a much more honest and just place than Heaven. She put down her empty glass of milk and thought that a Long Island Iced Tea would be nice. It was in her hand. She took it back into the living room and sat on the sofa with it. Lucifer hopped up with her.

"Don't you get hungry or anything?" she asked him.

"Not really, I am happy just to be here with you. I need nothing else," he replied, settling down next to her bare thigh. Buster had been insatiable, constantly begging for food and treats, hogging the bed, and demanding her attention. But only when it was inconvenient.

She took a sip of her drink. She had fucked an angel, but more than that, she had exposed a secret. The halos could be removed. And what happened then? Well pain had been the first lesson, but the sex. Fleeting sure, but that was only because the angel hadn't been altogether down with the act. Would they allow this breech of Heaven's façade to spread? She had thought of the sex as the naughty thing, but was telling people the truth actually the bigger violation? She remembered the man with a boner and his halo in his hand.

She sat for a while petting Lucifer and drinking her drink. The level of her drink getting no lower, although her buzz was intensifying. Lucifer had fallen asleep and was snoring. A little cat snore that made it hard for her to think of him as anything other than an actual cat. She got up, aware she was disturbing him and regretting it. Although, it wasn't like he would retaliate by puking in her shoe.

She walked into the room and opened her closet. The sun had gone down, and she thought she was ready for a night out. Gazing at her endless glittery robes, she grimaced. She took a really long drink this time and let the booze fuel her thoughts.

She ran her hands along the robes hanging in her closet. In Heaven where underwear was pointless and fashion not really even a thing, the existence of the closet seemed a little ridiculous. She spotted a dark green robe and plucked it off its hanger. She slipped it over her head. The hem lightly brushed the floor. She walked out of her closet.

"Stunning, Kat," said her butt hole-less cat.

"Why thank you, kind sir," she said and bowed.

She took yet another long slug of her drink. She was quite drunk now but was enjoying the feeling. She didn't feel like being sober, and she was about to face the angels who she was sure would be talking about what happened earlier that day. Maybe if she faced them hammered, she might be able to break through their smart-ass defenses. She hoped so. Her witty comebacks had been her claim to fame. At least she thought they had been. In Heaven, she was woefully under prepared for how to talk shit to angels. Maybe it was their damned halos.

She had snatched the hunky angel's halo. She did it right in front of him. Could she snatch the halos of the angels on the down low? Maybe she could collect them all before they knew what was happening. Or would it take them a while to figure it out? When their genitals returned? She wished she understood the logistics of Heaven a little better. The handbook hadn't covered halo theft. She would have to discover these things on her own.

"I think I'm going to steal their halos," she said to Lucifer. Her tongue was fat in her mouth, making her words sloppy. "Get them when they aren't looking."

"They're going to recognize you Kat," he said.

"You're right. How about now?" she went blonde.

"Better." Lucifer said. "But you still look like you."

Her brain was soaking in alcohol, and she was having trouble thinking. She set her drink down and got sober. She tried to change her face and couldn't. She wished it cleaned instead. No makeup.

"Ok how do I look?" she asked Lucifer.

"Pretty good I think," he replied, and she wondered if she should be trusting him.

He seemed to worship her, and she had no doubt that if she had put on a pair of jeans and asked him if her ass looked fat, he would say no. Even if they made her butt look the size of a mail truck. She checked herself out in the mirror for another assessment. She didn't like herself as a blonde, but she thought she might just get away with her little stunt.

Kat looked at the drink she had left on the nightstand. It was still full, and the ice hadn't melted at all. She took a long swallow. Just to take the edge off, now that she was ready, she was getting nervous. She took another long one for good measure and headed out toward the door, passing the kitchen on the way. *Ooo donut!* She resisted this time. Barely.

The night was beautiful, as expected. The stars were out, and the moon hung in the sky like a big yellow halo. Kat was excited. She suspected this might be a bad idea. If the word had gotten around about what happened earlier, they might just see her coming. But at least she was doing something. And not just sitting in her house and getting fucked up and eating donuts for all of eternity. Although as a backup plan, it didn't sound too bad. *No, that was Heaven talking. Nice try, though, with the booze and the donuts.*

She heard the bar before she saw it. It sounded like heavy metal. Sort of. The closer she got the more the music sounded familiar. She stopped to listen. As had happened with Dahmer, the recognition was slow in coming, but when it did, it hit her like a falling piano. Stryper. *What the actual fuck?* And that was the last of her doubts about going to Hell. Burning forever was preferable than listening to even one Stryper song. Although she had to admit, it was at least better than country music. But not by much.

As painful as it was, she started walking again toward the unimaginably terrible music. The bar looked different from last time. Colored lights, streamers, and balloons hung from the ceiling. Birthday party? Couldn't be. A celebration of someone getting to Heaven, maybe. Death party? That seemed more likely. *How morbid.* If she did her job right, they might just make a holiday of out of the day she got sent to Hell. She hadn't made much of a mark on earth; it would be cool to leave such a mark in Heaven.

As she got closer, she saw the reason. Jesus. What was it his birthday? She didn't think it was Christmas, but she had yet to see a calendar, so she really didn't know. He was standing on the bar and saying weird shit. Mercifully, the music stopped.

"Rejoice in the Lord always; again, I will say, Rejoice." Jesus said. He was looking at the ceiling of the bar and not at the faces looking up at him.

They were just rejoicing for the hell of it. Cool. Not one of them had noticed Kat. The ones who had glanced her way showed no recognition or animosity. So far, so good. She saw the pale angel up in the front row. The crowd of angels was quite large, but all of them were paying attention to Jesus. Some of them held wine glasses and others what looked like mixed drinks. Catholics sure liked their booze, dead or alive.

Kat walked casually to the back of the row and tilted her head up toward Jesus. Amazing at how uninterested he was in the people who were so enamored with him. He seemed to be in his own little world. Which was awesome for Kat, because he was the only one in a position to see her without turning his head. She crept up to the nearest angel, a guy with brown skin and dark hair. He had tears in his eyes. She stood up on her tiptoes to reach his head. She turned her head both ways to make sure no one was watching her. Nope, all teary eyes on Jesus.

"The thief comes only to steal and kill and destroy. I came that they may have life and have it abundantly." Jesus called from the top of the bar.

Wait what? Alarmed, Kat dropped back down on her flat feet. But when she looked around, there was still no one looking at her. Jesus continued.

"If I speak in the tongues of men and of angels, but have not love, I am a noisy gong or a clanging cymbal. And if I have prophetic powers, understand all mysteries and all knowledge, and if I have all faith, so as to remove mountains, but have not love, I am nothing. If I give away all I have, and if I deliver up my body to be burned, but have not love, I gain nothing. Love is patient and kind; love does not envy or boast; it is not arrogant or rude. It does not insist on its own way; it is not irritable or resentful."

Cool, he was talking about himself, again. She darted her hand up and snatched the halo off the angel. She brought it down and held it by her side. The guy shuffled his feet, but otherwise didn't seem to notice. She wondered if he had a tingle in his crotch.

She waited a few moments, pretending to be paying attention to the dude talking. She could not produce the tears in her eyes, but it didn't appear that any of them were watching her that closely. She noticed that most of them did not have their wings. She could relate, they were not as cool as one would think.

The now halo-less guy still hadn't noticed, so Kat looked around for her next mark. She spotted a short brunctte in a golden robe. She crept up behind her and lifted her halo off her head with all the grace and ease of a gentle lover. There seemed to be a bit of a trick to removing the halos. A little twist to the side and she didn't feel that strange resistance to taking it off. The brunette kept staring at Jesus. Kat had stopped listening to Him, but kept her gaze on Him anyway. She had learned that lesson in church. She had tuned out all but the loudest of the priest's ramblings.

Kat moved on, and before long, she was holding more than a dozen golden rings. She was feeling conspicuous now. The jig would be up if anyone saw her holding them. She lifted her robe and pinned them between her thighs.

The crowd had begun to grow a little restless, Jesus did not notice. He was still going on, something about a fat calf or whatever. They were rustling around, the ones whose halos she had pilfered were moving around anxiously, looking like they had to pee. The first one she had robbed was looking around now, looking really nervous. She looked down and was impressed by the size of the protrusion in the front of his robe. It might be time to take her goods and get the hell out of there. Shit looked like it was about to get real.

A low mumbling started to roll through the crowd as some of the angels began to notice they didn't feel quite like angels anymore. One of them, the short brunette had dropped her robe. She had caught sight of the tented robe and was moving toward him. He dropped his robe, they began to make out, and soon they were doing much more than that.

Kat moved toward the exit, but the halos she had between her legs were making it hard to walk.

"Hey! You!" she heard someone yell, when she turned to look, it was Lyla.

Kat gave up trying to hide the halos and let them drop out of the bottom of her robes. They clattered to the ground. The blonde angel moved toward her but was thwarted by a previously haloed lady on her knees trying to swallow the newly restored erection of a lovely looking gentleman. This was devolving into a heavenly orgy. Kat started to run back home as she changed her hair back to its original color. Lyla turned her attention back to the bar patrons and looked to have given up pursuit, Kat could hear her yelling at them to stop doing what they were doing.

Jesus, oblivious to the activities of his audience, was still preaching, "A new command I give you: Love one another. As I have loved you, so you must love one another." His audience was certainly taking his advice.

129

Chapter 16

Kat burst through her gate and front door. Lucifer was already awake and waiting for her. She didn't wait for him to ask her how it went.

"Holy shit. I took a butt load of halos. They didn't even notice, and then they all started fucking each other. If that doesn't get me thrown out of Heaven, I don't know what will," she said. "But even if I get stuck here, at least I spread some truth and joy."

She was almost breathless, from the excitement and the run home. Lucifer looked impressed.

"That's great, you're still here though," he said, a mournful look on his face. "Kat, what happens to me if you go to Hell?"

"I don't really know buddy. I don't know if I can take you with me, but I'm totally winging it here. The demon said that stuff that goes through the portal gets all fucked up. I wouldn't want that to happen to you. I wouldn't want it to happen to me either for that matter, or I would just try to go with him." She thought for a moment," Maybe you need to get kicked out too?"

"Ok. I don't know what would happen if you left me. I

only exist because of you," he said.

Kat bristled a little at the guilt trip, but she still felt bad for letting Buster down.

"I promise to do what I can, little dude. I think from now on you'll need to be my partner in crime," Kat said, and Lucifer looked pleased. She hoped she could deliver on that promise.

As she pictured the scene she had created, she thought she would like to lose her halo for good. The angels were certainly having fun without theirs. She reached up and gave it a little twist. It didn't budge. Weird. She tried again. Same thing. Now she was getting pissed. She had just stolen at least a dozen and now hers wouldn't come off. She grabbed the thing with both hands, tilted it to the side and pulled as hard as she could. It stuck fast. She looked around the room for something to help her. A crowbar appeared in her hand. She hooked the halo with one end and wrenched down with the other. Amazed by her newfound supernatural strength, she flipped ass over face and landed on her back on the floor. Halo still firmly over her head. Once again, she was faced with an unwelcome epiphany. Instead of sending her to Hell, they stuck the fucking halo to her head with some sort of divine super glue. This was officially war.

Kat went into her room to retrieve her pipe. It was late, but she didn't feel like sleeping. No longer expecting a knock on her door at any moment. They weren't going to send her to Hell, just sentence her to an eternity without a pussy. She dropped her robe on the floor and laid down on her bed. Lucifer came and joined her.

She wished she had stayed instead of running, but Lyla scared her. Like a middle school bully, she probably had no power at all, but Kat was frightened of her, anyway. She lit her pipe and discovered it was empty. She reached to repack it and saw she was down to her last bowl. It was a pity the bag didn't refill itself like the alcohol did. Dejected, she willed herself to sleep with her not quite cat next to her.

When she woke, still naked on top of her covers, the sun was shining through her window. *Still in Heaven,* she thought with dismay. *Fuck.* Lucifer saw that she was awake and perked up.

"Good morning, Kat," he said.

"Good morning to you too," she replied, only somewhat amazed at how easy it was to get used to a talking cat. Never mind the not eating or pooping thing, the talking thing was definitely more than a little weird.

She lay there a moment and was about to reach for her pipe, when she remembered she was out. Lame. She was going to get up and get some coffee, but as the thought came, a steaming mug with just the right amount of milk and sugar appeared on her bedside table. She sat up and took a sip. She hoped the coffee was this good in Hell, but even if it weren't, the shitty blonde angel wouldn't be there. And that would be worth bad coffee for the rest of eternity.

"Well, I got to go get more weed," she said to Lucifer. "I think from now on you need to stay with me. If I ever get sucked down to Hell, I'll have a better chance of hanging on to you."

Lucifer said nothing, but he smiled kind of. A weird cat approximation of a smile which bared his fangs. She had changed her mind about getting rid of him, weird as he was. She just hoped something fucked up wouldn't happen to him on the way to Hell. Assuming she could get there at all. She was starting to have doubts. But the events of the night before strengthened her resolve.

It would be nice to talk to Amon again at least. She couldn't wait to tell him about screwing Chad the Admin angel, stealing the halos and inducing an orgy. She didn't bother picking out a new robe and just picked up the one off the floor and slipped it over her head. Kat supposed if her crotch wasn't as smooth and round as a bald guy's head she wouldn't even bother. But she was far more embarrassed by her lack of genitals than by exposing them.

Lucifer followed her out of her bedroom, hanging just a little too close than she would have preferred. It was almost the most catlike thing he had done, but the illusion fell apart when he made sure not to get in the way and trip her. She made her way to her front door. *Ooo donut!* She stuffed one in her mouth as she stepped outside. She forgot for a moment that Lucifer was behind her and almost caught his tail in the door.

"Sorry, dude. I'm going to have to get used to you following me," she said, the strange cat just gave her his weird smile. It would have given her the creeps, except that she knew he meant well.

They started along the path to the waterfall. She hoped she could find it. It did not seem like a place that encouraged visitors, considering it was the portal to Hell and all. Soon though, she heard the water and made her way through the dense forest. Lucifer had an easier time of it, being much smaller than she was. The beauty of the waterfall shocked her, as it had the first time. The rainbow still hung over the spot where the water tipped over the edge. The only animal in the area was her Lucifer.

She spotted the fruit trees and realized she should have brought something to put them in. A basket appeared in her hand, as convenient as just wishing things into existence was. She didn't think she would ever quite get used to it. She barely had to try anymore. Things just came. She picked a bunch more fruit than she had last time and saved one for herself. She then picked up a pebble to toss in the space between the rocks.

Lucifer followed her to the spot but looked to be a

little fearful. She set down the basket and tossed the pebble into the hole. Lucifer let out a little whine, and she picked him up to cradle him in her arms. He licked her face.

"It's cool. Amon is a good dude. He won't hurt you, but he is a little scary to look at. If you think you're going to freak out, you can go chill over there by that tree, but stay close," she said. Lucifer nuzzled a little closer against her shirt.

When Amon failed to materialize, she looked around for another pebble to throw. Still holding her scared kitty, she bent down and picked one up by her feet. She threw it into the hole as she had the last time, but she didn't hear it bounce down into the rocks.

"What the fuck?" Amon said.

The wolf demon poked his head through the opening and belched a large flame. She saw he had a little red spot in the middle of his forehead.

"That hurt, man. I heard you the first time, you got to give me a minute," he said.

"I'm sorry. It burned you?" she asked. Lucifer had stiffened in her arms and was trembling.

"Yeah, stuff from Heaven doesn't agree with me. Except for that fruit. I guess that is your Heaven cat. Don't worry. I won't hurt you. I only look like a wolf here. In Hell, I look more like a regular guy. Not handsome, but not this wolf looking thing I am here. God's idea of a nasty joke, I guess," Amon said to Lucifer.

"This is Lucifer," she said, Lucifer seemed to relax a little.

"Ha! Good name. You need more weed?" Amon said.

"I do, I brought you more fruit."

"Sweet," he said. Amon disappeared for a moment, and when he returned, he was holding a big bag of pot. Kat moved the basket close to him and he brought it into the hole with him. He touched a few before deciding on which one to eat first. Kat thought this was a little silly as they were all perfect.

It wasn't like he was going to find one that wasn't ripe or bruised.

"I'm pretty sure they're all the same," she said, taking a seat on the stone and packing her pipe.

"Force of habit, I guess most of the fruit is bruised in Hell. You got to really dig for the good ones," he said, taking a huge bite and baring his vicious looking teeth.

Kat set Lucifer down on the stone, and he curled up in her lap. Relaxed, but kept an eye on the demon. Amon was relishing his fruit. Kat looked away as the juice dripped off his furry jaw. The sight of the wolf demon devouring the fruit was gruesome. It was too easy for her to imagine him sinking those same fangs into flesh.

"Did you change your mind about coming to Hell?" he asked.

"No, I've been trying. No luck. I had sex with an angel, though. And I stole a bunch of halos and they all just started fucking. Without the halos everyone's genitals come back. I don't know if they realized they were gone, or just didn't care. It was quite the sight, but now my own halo won't come off." She said, taking a tremendous hit and blowing the smoke toward the demon.

"That sounds pretty cool. I wish I could've seen it. I bet you'll fit right in down in Hell," he said. He had made his way to the bottom of the basket. "I got to go. I was in the middle of a wicked chess game with some physicist. That fucker thinks he's so smart. See you later, good luck," Amon waved his paw and ducked down into the hole.

Kat sat for a little while and smoked some more. Lucifer hopped off her lap, and he was sniffing around the grass and the trees. She realized that this was the first time he had been anywhere other than her house. As he sniffed around, a leaf drifted down from a nearby tree, and he paused. Staring at the leaf, he lowered his front half to the ground, as his back half started to wiggle. He sprang at the leaf and caught it in his jaws. He trotted over to her and dropped the leaf at her feet. He looked up at her and gave her his best cat smile. His lips bared his little fangs. Kat giggled and patted his head. There was no way she could leave him here.

"Good job, little dude!" She said, "let's head home, I'll get you a couple of toys and we can play."

She stood up and they started the walk home. She took a bite of the fruit she had picked for herself and hoped she didn't look as menacing as the demon had as the juice ran down her chin.

"It's too bad you can't eat dude, this is delicious," she said through a mouthful of orange fruit.

"I could try," Lucifer said. Kat thought about this, if she could enjoy food, why not her cat. She wished for a bag of cat treats. She dropped the piece of fruit when the bag of cat treats appeared in her hand. She stopped and held one out to Lucifer, who seemed leery at first. Like he didn't quite know what to do with it. He took it gently from her fingers and chewed. His eyes lit up.

"Oh wow! This is awesome! Can I have more?" He was hopping up and down. She gave him another, and he took it greedily. "I love you," he said after he finished.

The smile he had been wearing faded from his face, replaced by a look of alarm. He sat down and looked under his tail. Kat looked too. She had little choice, as he was displaying it prominently. He acquired a butt hole. Balls too if she wasn't mistaken. Yet another revelation. Feed the animals in Heaven, and they get their buttholes back.

"It's alright, dude. I promise," she said, and she bent down to pat his head.

"Did you see it though? I mean really look at it," Lucifer had turned his hind end to her with his tail as high as it could go. "Really, look at it. LOOOOOOK!"

"Yeah, I know. It's a butthole," Kat rolled her eyes as she stood up. "Come on, let's go home."

Kat and Lucifer walked home. Lucifer didn't walk so much as bounce. This whole time she had been assuming that all of his pleasure came from pleasing her. It made her happy to see him so pleased with himself. She was going to give him all the food when they got home.

She did exactly that when they got home. She got Lucifer a food dish and filled it with the foulest smelling cat food she could muster, which was pretty fucking foul. He smashed his face into the dish and when he raised his head, the brown mush covered his face. He splattered all around his dish on the floor of the kitchen. At least for a few moments. It disappeared as soon as she saw it. She wondered how long it would be before she would need to get him a litter box. She frowned, but the frown ran away from her face as she watched Lucifer lick his paw and groom his face.

She grabbed the box of non-abrasive Captain Crunch and took it to her sofa. She packed another bowl and wished for music. But realized her mistake as Brad Paisley began praising God in his country drawl. Horrified, she willed it to stop. Lucifer hopped up on the couch with her. She took a long hit off her pipe, followed by a handful of cereal. Lucifer was grooming the rest of his body.

"Want to try some pot?" She asked. She had never blown smoke in Buster's face because it was a dick move, but Lucifer wasn't an actual cat as far as she knew. And it was always better to get stoned with a buddy.

"Sure," he said, mid-lick, his tongue still sticking out. She took another long hit and blew the smoke in his face. Lucifer's eyes drooped, and she was afraid she had made a mistake.

"I like that a lot," he said, his words slow and drawn

out.

The two of them melted into the sofa. After a while, Lucifer got up and walked a little closer to her, turned around, and lifted his tail.

"Hey, I want to show you something," he said.

Chapter 17

"Ok, so we are going to need to have a talk about your new butthole, little dude," Kat said.

"It's great, isn't it?" Lucifer said.

"Uh, sure, but I've already seen it. I don't need to see again," she said, trying to be patient. She could relate to discovering body parts she thought she wouldn't see again, but this was getting ridiculous.

"What if it changes or does something cool, though? You will definitely want to see it then, right?" he replied.

"I have some experience with butt holes, if it changes or does something 'cool' then I really don't want to see it," she said. This time she couldn't help but roll her eyes. When she first met the creature, his un-catlike behavior had disturbed her, but the more he acted like an actual cat, the more she rethought that sentiment. She almost wished his new body part away. But when she looked at him, he seemed so happy she just couldn't do it. "Just let me know if you have to poop, I'll get you a litter box."

"What's poop?" he asked.

"Well after you eat, your body turns that food into poop and it comes out…" she hesitated, ready to change the subject. He might be even more excited to put the thing in her face if he understood its intended function. "Your butt hole," Kat cringed.

"Wow. That sounds cool. Do you poop?" he asked.

She rolled her eyes, "Not in Heaven. You know now that I think about it, you probably won't either. Your butt hole is probably just for show." She regretted the words as soon as they left her mouth.

"Oh really," he turned his hind end to her again.

"No! I've seen it. No more of that. Save it for people who haven't seen it yet. Ok, that's enough cat butt for today," she scowled at him to let him know she was serious. He dropped his head.

"Sorry," he said, and now she felt bad.

"It's cool. I'm just not that into cat ass. Hey, how about some more treats?" she said and watched him perk up.

She took out the bag of treats and fed him one at a time. He seemed to forget all about showing her his new butt, for now. She suspected this was going to be an ongoing issue.

As Kat watched him gobble his treats, she thought she might want one too. The pot here gave her the wicked munchies. She thought about what she wanted. Chips, soda, chocolate, and then an idea hit her.

"Hey, how about we take all our junk food where everyone can see it. It could be a fine display of gluttony," Lucifer looked dubious, obviously happy getting stoned and eating right here on the couch. "You could show off your new butt hole." That got his attention.

"That sounds like a fine idea," he said.

"Cool, let's go," Kat said, and had to peel herself off the sofa. It was tempting to just sit here and smoke, eat, and talk to her cat. Heaven was always trying to knock her off course. She would resist. In a moment. She sank back down and smoked another bowl. She didn't want to take her weed with her, lest she lose it. If she couldn't get out of here, forever would be much easier with marijuana. Now that she couldn't remove her halo, she suspected if they found out about the weed, they might ruin that for her too. And who knows what might happen to Amon. He was really starting to grow on her.

She was still trying to gather her motivation when Lucifer nudged her, bumping his head against her thigh.

"Come on, let's go," he said. He was hopping up and down again.

She got up for real this time and headed for the door. Lucifer followed. When she stepped out onto her porch, Jeffrey was staring into her yard. Wearing his blank face that was almost as disturbing as his smile. He waved. She frowned and flipped him off. Lucifer, taking his cue, turned his back to him and lifted his tail. Kat couldn't tell if he was trying to offend him or show off his butt. Jeffrey frowned back and ducked back into his house, to do God knows what. Come to think of it, did God know what people did in their houses in Heaven? Does he know and not care, or does he prefer to stay ignorant? She thought it might be the latter, considering that doing those things in public seemed to be a faux pax.

As soon as she walked through her gate, cat in tow, she let Jeffery slip from her mind. Righteously stoned and thinking about all the things she wanted to put in her mouth. Pancakes, cookies, and saltine crackers with peanut butter. Once when she had been a teenager, she had gotten high and had put so many crackers into her spitless mouth she had almost choked. She had spat the dry wad of chewed crackers out onto the carpet of her best friend's bedroom. Her friend was laughing too hard to be upset. Here in Heaven, where the coffee was always perfect, and the donuts never stale, she wondered if that kind of thing could even happen.

They came across the platform where she had seen Jesus

speak. It appeared to be a gathering spot for angels and there were a few hanging around, being dicks, she was sure. They paid her no attention when she and Lucifer jumped up on the stage and sat down. She materialized a couple of beanbag chairs, a large blue one for her, and a small green one for Lucifer. The way they were ignoring her, she thought they might not have suspected that it was her who had caused the impromptu orgy at Jesus' Ted talk last night. She wasn't sure if that was a good thing or not, she was trying to get thrown out of Heaven. She might need to make sure she received the credit for that.

First, she made sure that Lucifer had as much food as he could scoop up with his mouth. She produced a huge cat dish filled with all manner of disgusting cat delicacies. Then she started on her own. A large box of crackers and tub of peanut butter appeared beside her. She pulled out a cracker and dipped it in, before stuffing the whole thing in her mouth. Then another and another. Soon she had a huge ball of dry paste in her mouth that she was unable to swallow. *That answers that question,* she thought, and a glass quart bottle of milk appeared. She took a long drink and swallowed.

Next, a chocolate layer cake. A few of the angels milling around shot looks of contempt in her direction, but still seemed like they were trying to ignore her. She smiled at them through a mouthful of cake. She made sure not to let all of it make it into her mouth. She let the frosting smear on her cheeks and chin. Smashing into her mouth like a groom into the mouth of his blushing bride.

Then some potato chips, the crumbs now sticking to the frosting. She was having a good time. Lucifer was still ass up, face down in his dish. He was eating like a pig and showing off his butt. Impressed by his efficiency, she moved on to a large roast turkey leg. She brought the thing up to her mouth and tore at it with her teeth. The crowd of angels had grown thicker now, most of them having a hard time ignoring her disgusting show.

Crumbs and bits of food now covered her robe, and she thought she could feel it tightening. That couldn't be, could it? Could she get fat in Heaven? She hadn't eaten more than an earth's meal worth since coming to Heaven. She didn't get full really but hadn't felt the need to eat much more than what she might have on earth. She looked over to Lucifer and thought he looked a little plumper.

"How you doing, buddy?" she asked him through a mouthful of double stuffed Oreos. He lifted his face from his bowl, and he was coated in a meaty mess of cat food. It covered his face from his ears to his neck.

"Pretty good, you got anything else?" he asked and indeed she did. She produced a treat dispenser and placed it next to his cat beanbag. He waddled over to it and slunk down. Positioning himself so that he could press the lever and get a morsel without moving from his spot. He didn't bother to clean his face, and the wet cat food was drying on his fur.

The angels were now stealing glances in their direction, unable to conceal their disdain. Kat kept on, now sure that her belly was expanding. Her vanity kicked in and she wondered if she wanted to ruin her perfect body. A sneer from a black-haired female angel, who looked familiar, convinced her she didn't give a shit. She could figure out how to lose it later. She held up a pink frosted donut and deadpanned the angel while thrusting her tongue in and out of the pastry's hole, sprinkles raining down on her shirt.

Her robe was becoming noticeably tighter. Lucifer's belly was expanding also, as he pressed the treat lever repeatedly. A look of contentment on his face. Her own belly was now protruding past her growing breasts. She must look disgusting. The angels were openly staring now and whispering to each other. The crowd getting larger.

Kat stuffed a foot-long hotdog smothered in chili and

cheese into her mouth, chili splattering on the front of her robe, which was now uncomfortably tight. She heard a loud rip as it split up the middle. There was a gasp from the crowd of horrified angels. Her boobs were glaring in defiance at the angels' outrage. She smiled through the melted cheese, beans and meat sticking to her cheeks.

She kept eating. A cheesecake now. She picked the whole thing up at once and took the largest bite her mouth would allow. Most of it not making it inside. The angels, clearly disturbed, turned to look at the arrival of Lyla.

"Lyla's here," she heard the dark-haired angel say.

She now held a large bag of peanut M&M's and was tossing them in the air and attempting to catch them with her mouth, with little success. She grabbed a handful and stuffed them into her mouth. She kept eye contact with Lyla as the colored sugar coating fell from her lips. She was chewing with her mouth open.

"What the fuck do you think you're doing, Kathy?" Lyla the angel said, glaring at her. Lucifer shifted in his beanbag, trying with great effort to dislodge himself. He had grown to the size of a small beach ball. He hoisted his weight up, and positioned himself to the edge of the stage with his back end to the crowd and lifted his tail.

"What do you think of this?" He asked. Alarmed, Lyla looked away, clutching at her neckline.

"We're just 'going forth and enjoying Heaven' as Jesus said. I've earned my divine reward, haven't I?" Kat said, spraying bits of peanuts and chocolate in the angel's direction. She smiled again. The chocolate had smeared on her front teeth, making it look like she was missing a couple.

"I know what you did last night," angel Lyla said, smirking.

"I know what I did too, I thought it was quite impressive," Kat said, holding a large double bacon cheeseburger in her hands. She mashed it into her face, biting off a bit, before holding the whole mess out to Lyla. The angel recoiled.

"I will not let this stand. You are welcome to your sin in your own home. I will not allow you to corrupt our heavenly beings this way. You disgust me, you stop this right now!" Lyla said, the crowd murmured in agreement.

Not breaking eye contact, Kat stuffed a huge handful of cheese puffs into her mouth. She understood her miscalculation as she tried to reply. Her mouth devoid of moisture, she coughed when she tried to speak and blew out a cloud of orange particles, hitting Lyla's face with the dust. She looked as if she had gotten a badly tinted spray tan. Kat burst out laughing at the sight. Her orange face underneath her yellow hair made her look ridiculous.

Lyla wiped her face with the handkerchief that had appeared in her hand and when she took it away, her face was as fresh as the heavenly dew. Kat didn't know if it was the weed, or her sudden extreme weight gain that caused her epiphany. But she no longer gave any fucks about this angel. She felt silly for harboring the slightest amount of fear of her at all.

"Well, what are you going to do about it? Tattle to God? Doesn't he know already? Besides, I'm only following Jesus' instructions. Speaking of, aren't you supposed to 'love thy neighbor' or some shit?" Kat said. She had a large bottle of water and had taken a drink to wet her parched mouth. Lucifer still had his ass to the crowd, now and then he would look behind to see if anyone were looking. No one was, they were too busy watching the confrontation between Kat and Lyla. Lucifer stayed strong though, resting his head on the stage while keeping his butt elevated.

"You won't be so smug when you get sent to Hell!" Lyla yelled, and the crowd behind her applauded.

"Oh yeah? Why don't you fucking try me?" Kat said,

impressed with her newfound ability to talk shit to this angel.

Lyla turned away from Kat and addressed her audience. "You all need to leave at once, pay no more attention to this obese whore!"

"Wow, fat shaming now, huh? That doesn't seem like the Christian thing to do now, does it. What would Jesus say?" Kat said and laughed again, this time with an empty mouth. "I think I'm about done here, anyway."

Pleased with the open revulsion on the angel's face. She attempted to rise from her beanbag and got only a few inches up before falling back into it. Lucifer trotted over as fast as he could, which wasn't fast at all, to see if he could help. He couldn't but he smiled at her in moral support. The crowd was dispersing now, muttering to each other as they left. She tried again to lift herself, this time wishing for a cane to help her. She made it to her feet. Her ruined robe fell to the stage as she stood up. Naked, she stepped down, finding it difficult to move her bulk. Lucifer hopped down and landed with a thud.

Kat considered using a scooter or a wheelchair of some type to get home but decided not to.

"Come on Lucifer, I think we could use a walk," she said.

They started on the walk home. Slowly at first, but as they walked the extra pounds melted away. By the time they got to the gate, they were both back to their normal sizes. Groovy.

Chapter 18

"That was a lot of fun," Lucifer said as they walked through the door. He hopped up on the sofa, still covered in cat food.

"It sure was. How about we get cleaned up?" Kat was about to suggest that they take a bath, but she wasn't sure how he was going to take that. She once tried to give Buster a bath, and that had ended with her bleeding and apologizing. But she didn't need to worry about it. As soon as she wanted him clean, he was. "Never mind then, I'm going to take a bath."

She padded into the bathtub and filled it up. She was clean too by that time, but she wanted to get in anyway. The scent of lavender and lilac filled the bathroom and she stepped into the tub. She remembered she had left her pipe and the bag of weed on her coffee table. Not wanting to get out, she called to her cat.

"Lucifer! Can you bring me the pipe and weed?" she said.

He came trotting in with both in his mouth.

"Can I have some too? I like that stuff," he said.

Kat looked at her bag, and it was getting low already.

"Sure, we're going to have to get more soon," Kat, said. She really preferred the weed over the booze.

She smoked in the tub and gloated over her performance that afternoon. Lucifer made the whole thing even better, she made sure to blow each new hit into his waiting face. As much as she missed Buster, she was enjoying Lucifer's company.

The thought of Buster in Hell led to thoughts of her mom. She hadn't thought of her for some time. She focused on her mother's face. It was swimming in and out of focus. Kat thought it might be the weed. She focused harder and was able to see her mother at her home. She was standing in her kitchen and looking at something in her hands. She was crying, softly. Kat dialed in and saw that in her mother's hands was a picture of herself.

The picture had been taken on the last Easter that she had spent while living at her mother's house. She had been 17 and was standing in front of her mother's church. It was also the last time she had been to a church. She tried to reach her mother; she had no doubt she was picturing her only daughter boiling in a lake of fire. Suffering. For a moment she felt she was standing in the kitchen next to her, she reached out with one hand to touch her. Kat's hand touched her mother's shoulder but moved right through it. Kat moaned, as she realized that she was unable to communicate. She was pulled back into the tub in Heaven. Tears filled her eyes and she let out a sob, but even in her pain, the tears would not fall.

Lucifer, having had enough of the smoke, had gone into the living room to take his spot on the couch. She suspected he was licking his butt.

"Kat!" he called, "something came under the door."

Before she could tell him to bring it to her, he was coming into the bathroom with a note in his mouth. He dropped it on the floor where she retrieved the folded piece of paper. It was written on the same paper that she had gotten from Chad the admin angel. She unfolded it and read the words written in irritatingly perfect cursive.

"Jesus has requested your presence in his office as soon as possible."

Could this be is it? Her ticket to Hell? She hopped out of the tub and didn't bother to dry off. She went to her closet to grab a robe. She took her pipe with her into the living room and took a puff before telling Lucifer of their invitation.

"Come on, we have a meeting with Jesus. I think this might be it. We could be going to Hell," she said to Lucifer. A hint of fear touching his eyes. "It's ok if you've changed your mind, I don't know what Hell is like exactly, I won't be mad if you don't want to go."

He paused for a moment and said, "But I don't know if I'll even exist here without you."

In another context, that may have sounded like the melodramatic words of a rejected lover. But she knew in his case, it might be true.

"I want you with me, but I think it's safe to say things won't be as easy there as they are here. If what Amon says is true, it's much more like real life, with pain and where everything is not perfect," she said, not really giving him an answer.

"Did you like life on earth?" He asked.

She paused with her hand on the door and stopped to think about it.

"You know, I did. Sure, there were troubles and sometimes things hurt, but I enjoyed my life. And I think that had a lot to do with the fact that I didn't expect there to be anything after. Here in Heaven, it's easy to take stuff for granted. Things on earth have more meaning and more enjoyment, if only because they aren't guaranteed. I didn't think that there was an afterlife, so I tried to enjoy my life as much as I could," she said. She hadn't been prepared for such an existential question from a talking cat in Heaven.

"I think I want to be with you Kat," he said.

She took a long puff off her pipe and blew it out the door as she walked out. The smoke billowed out and she saw Karen watching her.

"What is that? Pot smoke. Figures a slut like you would be a pothead too. Probably helps with anal!" Karen yelled from her yard, and Kat had to admit to herself that Karen wasn't totally wrong.

"Fuck you, kid killer," Kat yelled back before walking out of her gate to meet Jesus. *Isn't Heaven grand?*

It was getting late in the afternoon and the sun was starting to set. The colors in the sky were hard to ignore. Deep red and orange glowed on the horizon. She wanted to appreciate it before descending into Hell. She had no doubt that there were going to be some things she was going to miss about this place. She picked up Lucifer so that he could see it better. He said nothing as he gazed at the sky.

Soon they came to the Administration building. She still held Lucifer in her hands, afraid that if she were sent down and not holding him, he might be left behind. She still wasn't sure if he would go with her at all, but then again, she hadn't been sure of anything since popping into Heaven. She opened the large doors and walked toward Chad. He looked at her as if he had never seen her.

"Can I help you miss?" He said, and she thought she saw a glimmer of recognition in his eyes. It was hard to miss with his incessant eye contact.

"You already did," she replied and gave him a wink. "But I am here at the request of our lord and savior, Jesus Christ." Her tone dripped with condescension.

"Go on ahead, I'm sure he's expecting you," Chad said, still pretending to not know who she was.

She walked with her cat in her arms down the hallway to Jesus' stark office. She was getting nervous. This was probably going to hurt. She hoped Lucifer wouldn't be hurt too bad. She really hoped he wouldn't explode or something. His door was open, and he looked up as she approached the threshold.

"Hello, Kathy. Please come in and sit," Jesus said.

She did as he asked, setting Lucifer on her lap. "This is Lucifer, I won't let him leave my side," Kat said. Pronouncing the name with as much emphasis as he had used when calling her Kathy. He had no reaction to her choice of pet names, ever stoic, the dick.

"It has been brought to my attention that you have been acting out here in Heaven. We have provided all the things to keep you contented in your home and yet you insist on being a bother. You have been forgiven for your sins my child, your soul rests in Heaven," he said.

Kat didn't know what to say, did she double down? Did she confront the hypocrisy? Jesus had been easy to ignore when he was spouting his goofy stuff, in his own display of vanity no less, but now in his presence she wasn't sure what to say to him.

"The angels aren't very nice…Sir…Jesus," fuck, she still didn't know how to address the demi-god. "I just wanted to show them that I didn't care what they thought. Also, I don't really like it here. I don't think I want to stay."

His eyes darkened, but in such a way that one might not notice if they weren't paying attention, but when he spoke again, his tone had taken a dark turn as well.

"You don't like Heaven? That can't be, that isn't right. You would rather be in Hell with the unrepentant deviants?" His tone went from dark to frightening but His volume stayed the same. Kat was afraid and Lucifer was trembling in her lap.

"As opposed to the repentant deviants? Jesus Christ, I live next door to a serial killer!" Her fear wasn't enough to quell her anger. Her neighbor in Heaven killed, sodomized, and ate people on earth for fuck's sake. "I'm starting to think that Hell might not be what you make it out to be. Heaven sure isn't. It all feels fake, like a pretty funhouse. Full of mean tricks and lies." That should do it. Kat braces herself.

Jesus appeared to be losing his cool as well, "You cannot dictate the rules of Heaven or repentance! Leave me now!" He boomed and she waited for the burning pain.

She sat with her eyes closed holding her terrified almost cat waiting for fire or demons or something to take her to Hell. When moments passed without so much as a little burn, she dared to open one eye. Jesus was just staring at her. He waved an impatient hand, and she stood up, incredulous.

She walked home, unsure of what to do now. She had so been looking forward to Hell, but here she was walking back to her home. Utterly unpunished. Heaven was a bunch of bullshit. Lucifer was trailing behind her utterly unperturbed. He was just interested in being with her, and his new butthole. He was very interested in that.

"You know what? Fuck this," Kat said and stopped walking in the direction of her house. She turned instead to the stage where they had their gluttonous food fest.

"Where are we going Kat?" Lucifer asked.

"They want us to stay in our house and enjoy their bullshit, well we just won't. We don't need to eat or sleep or any of that. We'll just sit and do nothing. Show them that we don't need that stuff," she said.

"Well, ok. I guess if that's what you want," Lucifer said, not sounding happy about this idea at all.

They walked and sat down on the stage; she was glad that there were no angels there. They sat down and did nothing.

After a while, angel Lyla walked by with a gaggle of other angels.

"What are you doing here Kathy the whore?" Lyla quipped.

"I just decided I don't need any of Heaven's meaningless bullshit," Kat replied.

"Huh? Not even your marijuana?" Lyla's tone rose to a high pitch.

"What the fuck are you talking about?" Kat said, alarmed. How could she know about her weed? Her neighbor's stupid face came to mind.

"If you do ever go back to your house, you'll see it has been removed. Almost everything is allowed in Heaven, but not that," and the angel walked off with a smirk.

Kat ditched her plan of openly rejecting the joys offered to her in Heaven as she thought of her only pleasure from Hell. She grabbed up Lucifer and ran all the way back to her house to find that her weed was gone.

Chapter 19

"Can't we go get some more?" Lucifer asked as Kat paced her small living room.

"I hope so, but I can't be sure. Seems to be a running theme here. The only thing I'm sure about is that angels suck ass," Kat replied.

"What's wrong with sucking ass? I have been enjoying licking mine," Lucifer said.

"I didn't really mean it that way, more like they are just shitty," Kat said, wanting to elaborate on the nuance, but not wanting to risk another butthole discussion with her cat.

"Let's go see if we can get some more pot," Kat said.

"It's dark outside, shouldn't we wait until morning?" Lucifer asked.

"I don't see why we should. It's not like we need to sleep, and I don't think demons keep business hours," Kat replied.

Kat and Lucifer stepped out into the night. The moon was shining, the sky was clear, and the stars were out in full force. She told herself that as lovely as the sky was, it wasn't earth's sky. Just like her cat, it was an approximation of what they saw on earth. As pretty as it was, she didn't trust it. It was just one more trick to add to the illusion.

As before, she heard the waterfall before she saw it, the trees were much harder to navigate in the darkness. She thought about obtaining a flashlight, but she didn't want to attract any attention. She still didn't know how much of what she thought or did was being monitored. It took her much longer to get through, but she did make it to the other side. Lucifer helped, as cats had on earth, he saw much better in the dark than humans.

She went to the fruit tree and began to gather some. She picked up the skirt of her robe to hold it. She found she wasn't as interested in saving a piece for herself. Heaven was losing its luster.

She made her way to the pile of stones, which disguised the portal to Hell. She sat down so she could hold the fruit while she looked for a pebble to throw. Lucifer sat down next to her, but not as close to the space where the demon would appear. Kat tossed a pebble and waited. And waited. She was about to reach for another pebble to throw but thought better of it. She didn't know if it was nighttime in Hell too, or if anyone slept there for that matter, but she wanted to stay in Amon's good graces. He was her contact in Hell, burning him again didn't seem like a smart thing to do. So, she waited. Finally, she heard shuffling and Amon poked his head out.

"So soon?" He said. There was no fire that came out with his words, just a foul stench. "I was sleeping." Kat recoiled at the demon's morning breath, hoping that Hell had toothbrushes.

"Yeah, someone ratted me out and it was gone. Although to be honest, I was getting low anyway. Sorry to wake you. I didn't know if it was nighttime there too, or if you even slept. I don't sleep unless I want to," Kat said, she started to place the fruit in her lap in a little pile by the hole.

"Sleeping, like eating, is something most of the creatures do in Hell," he looked at the fruit. "You know, I don't think I'm hungry right now. I ate so much the other day, but I'll get you another sack anyway. I knew angels were assholes, but to take your weed. That just sucks. You can't steal in Hell," he said. "Well, you can, but the punishment isn't worth it. Trust me," and he disappeared for a minute. He returned a few seconds later with a large sack of pot and another pipe. "Here you go, you know, maybe I'll have just one piece." He took a piece of fruit and took a large bite.

Kat found he wasn't quite as scary as he had been the last time. She was becoming accustomed to demons, which could only be a good thing if she ever made it to Hell. She had growing doubts that she would though. Lucifer seemed more relaxed too, even as he kept his eyes on the beast.

She took the pipe and weed, and slipped it into the pocket of her robe. She was ready to go home now. She found that she did want to sleep, or at least lay down for a while. Her body may not need it, but her mind could use a rest. She had been so wrapped up in her mission that she was ready for just a little down time. Some smoke would help her recharge and with a fresh mind she might just be able to come up with a plan that would work this time.

"If I leave it here, will you be able to come back and get it?" She asked Amon, who had finished his fruit.

"I'm not sure. I can't take it with me. Your Aunt Judy is due for another sack soon. She'll bring me more. She's still a little afraid of me. Could you tell her to chill if you see her?" He said.

Kat was touched that he was so concerned about Aunt Judy's fear. For a demon from Hell, he was a pretty nice dude. A little rough on the eyes maybe, but a good dude.

"Aunt Judy got really upset when I said I wanted to find you. She is afraid, not enough to stop smoking pot, but enough. I wish I could help, but I don't want to upset her again. Is there something you could do about the fire puke, or your face?" She cringed as the words came out of her mouth. "Sorry, that wasn't nice. But it is a little off putting."

As Amon laughed, flames and smoke came bellowing out of the space between the stones. Lucifer backed away. "That's all Heaven's doing, you'll have to talk to the man in charge about that. I swear I'm not this bad in my own space," he said. "Bye Kat."

"Smell ya later!" Kat called to him as he retreated to Hell. She cringed again, on earth that had been a term of endearment when saying goodbye to a friend, but she would never say it to someone who actually smelled bad. Her demon etiquette needed some work.

Kat and Lucifer made their way back to Kat's house. She walked in the door and sat down on the sofa passing the box of donuts in the kitchen, like the fruit they had lost some of their appeal as well. She reached into her pocket to retrieve her bounty. She couldn't feel it. She reached farther, and still nothing. She stood up and dropped her robe to the floor, expecting the goods to fall out. When they didn't, she got on her hands and knees and searched the cloth. She stood up: shaking it, hoping when the pipe fell out it wouldn't shatter. But still there was nothing.

"Son of a bitch," she said. Lucifer stared at her from his spot on the sofa with concern.

She had it when she was sitting by the stones. She thought she would have felt it drop while they were walking.

"God damn it," Kat said. "I either lost it, or it didn't make it out of the forest. I'm thinking it didn't make it out. I wonder if Aunt Judy still has hers. I hope so."

"It sounds like there's plenty of that stuff in Hell," Lucifer said, trying to be helpful.

"Yeah, if we ever get there. They didn't teach me how hard it would be to get to Hell in church, quite the opposite," she replied, and then patted his head. "I'm sorry, I'm just bummed. In the morning, we'll go visit Aunt Judy and see if she still has hers. I'll feel better if I know I didn't screw it up for her too."

She walked into her bedroom, and Lucifer followed. She laid down for a while and watched as the sunlight creeped in through her window. Lucifer had fallen asleep and was making small snoring sounds. She looked at him. He was so cute. If she loved anything in Heaven besides her aunt and father, it was this weird little cat.

When it was light enough outside, she got up and picked out a robe. Lucifer noticed she was up and was watching as she emerged from the closet.

"Good morning," he said.

"Good morning, little dude. Let's go see my aunt. Fair warning though, she has a ton of cats. Be nice," she said.

"Why wouldn't I be nice?" Lucifer asked.

"Cats don't always get along with other cats, so just be cool," she replied, and he nodded, still looking a little perplexed.

They set out on yet another gorgeous day in Heaven. As she opened her gate, she thought a bike might be cool. And a black bicycle with a blanket-lined basket attached to the handlebars appeared. She picked up Lucifer, who rather than being scared, was eager to sit in the basket.

"What is this?" he asked with wide eyes.

"A bicycle. We're going to go for a ride," she said and giggled.

She got on and started to peddle. Lucifer had put his front paws on the edge of the basket and was almost standing up. She could see his tongue was hanging out.

"I have to be able to see. Sit down little goofball," she said, and he did as he was asked.

They rode for a while, Lucifer having the time of his little life, and Kat found something else she enjoyed in Heaven. The wind in her hair as the trees blew past. The cobblestone road was less bumpy than she would have expected. The whole experience was delightful. So much so that she was miles past her aunt's house before she remembered that was where she had been going. She was about to stop and turn around, but Lucifer was looking more like a dog than a cat with his tongue hanging out of his mouth and wind in his fur. She decided it wouldn't hurt to go a little farther.

The landscape had changed, the houses grew sparse and then stopped all together. She hadn't seen a single soul since setting out that morning. She had gotten used to that. She thought Heaven would be so much more enjoyable if she had the chance to be social. Talk to people. There must be some cool people here.

The cobblestone road had ended, and she was on packed dirt now. The ride was smoother now. Lucifer showed no signs of boredom. She was also intrigued by this unexplored piece of Heaven. She had no reason to stop. It wasn't like Aunt Judy was going anywhere.

She noticed she was now on a slight incline. As the hill got steeper, she saw that she was coming into a valley. A large field of green grass was flanked by trees, and there looked to be a group of people standing and watching someone talk. Kat was getting excited now. What was this she had discovered?

She was close enough now to hear the speaker's voice, but not close enough to make out just what he was saying. Her optimism for finding friends waned as she sped toward the crowd. Her curiosity kept her going though. The guy talking looked familiar, but she was still too far away to see for sure. He spoke in short harsh bursts. She was now close enough to hear what he was saying, and she brought the bike to an abrupt stop. Lucifer caught himself right before he was flung from his basket.

"What the hell?" he said.

"Shhh…" she replied.

She was still a good thirty feet from the crowd of maybe 20 or so people and they hadn't noticed her presence. But she was sure they wouldn't be the kind of people that she would want to hang with. Nope, definitely not.

"Jesus has given the ultimate gift of redemption, and he finds the most joy in those deemed irredeemable. We are the chosen ones. God's favorites."

"Jesus confirms this in his own words when he said, 'What man of you, having a hundred sheep, if he has lost one of them, does not leave the ninety-nine in the open country, and go after the one that is lost, until he finds it? And when he has found it, he lays it on his shoulders, rejoicing. And when he comes home, he calls together his friends and his neighbors, saying to them, 'Rejoice with me, for I have found my sheep that was lost.' Just so, I tell you, there will be more joy in Heaven over one sinner who repents than over ninety-nine righteous persons who need no repentance.'

My followers rejoice! For we have been forgiven and have earned the right to enjoy all of Heaven!"

The crowd cheered and then stuck their right arms in the air, hands pointed straight in a salute to the man speaking. Then in unison, they cried "Praise God! Heil Hitler!"

"Holy fucking shit!" Kat whispered, feeling a little stupid for missing the tiny black mustache and anal-retentive hair do. "We got to get the fuck out of here."

She turned the bike around to face the steep hill. Coming down, she had not considered that she would have to get back up the fucking thing. She peddled as hard as she could and made her way slow at first but began to pick up speed. Physics in Heaven allowed her to get up the hill without as much effort as she had thought it would. On earth, she would have collapsed from exhaustion by now. Soon she was at the top. She looked back and was relieved to see that she had made it out unnoticed.

"Who is Hitler?" Lucifer asked when he saw that Kat was done with her panic.

"He killed like 6 million people on earth. A real bad dude," she said, deliberately understating the guy. "He must have repented before he died. Holy shit." Kat was still trying to process what she had just witnessed.

They peddled on the way they had come. The cobblestone road appeared and then the houses. The farther away she got the better she felt. But she was now convinced that Heaven had some fucked-up priorities.

Chapter 20

When they got to Aunt Judy's house, Kat's shock had subsided. Not much but a little. What the fuck was the point of Heaven if you could murder six million people and still get in? She was always reminded of her own transgressions and redemption. She was told not to judge others. It wasn't her place. She had tried to see it from that point of view, but she was done trying. Her own sins were miniscule compared to what God had forgiven. She was done being told that she shouldn't judge. Well, Kat was judging. She was judging hard.

She wanted to check in on Aunt Judy and see if she had screwed up the weed for everyone and not just herself. They had taken the weed, but they hadn't found out about Amon, unless they just didn't care. But Kat found it hard to believe that they would be cool with heavenly beings consorting with demons. Although if they were cool with Hitler, who could be sure what they were cool with?

She parked her bike and walked up to her aunt's door with Lucifer in tow. She knocked lightly on the door and waited. When there was no response, she knocked again, harder.

Their bike ride must have been longer than she thought because the sun was creeping low in the sky. She was just about to knock again when the door opened.

"Why hellllloooooo!" Aunt Judy slurred. "I'm's so happpppy to ssee you. Come in."

"Hi, Aunt Judy, this is Lucifer," Kat said, nodding to her little black and white cat by her feet.

"Hi," Lucifer said.

"Whoaa, your cat can talk?" Aunt Judy said as they walked through the door.

"Yeah, I was lonely, and wished he could talk. Now he does," Kat replied, following her to the sofa in the living room. Aunt Judy's cats parted to let them pass.

"I should do that!" Aunt Judy almost yelled. She was inebriated and was having trouble regulating her volume. Kat looked at the 25 or so cats and thought it would be a bad idea if they could all talk. "I don't have any pot, if that's what you are looking for," Aunt Judy said, this time in a tone so low it was almost a whisper. "I woke up and mine was missing. I went and got more from the demon, but it disappeared when I left the forest. So, I got drunk. Do you want a drink?"

"I'm ok. That sucks Auntie," Kat said, guilt creeping up into her voice. "Well, how have you been?" Kind of a dumb question considering they were supposed to be in paradise.

In addition to finding out whether or not she had fucked up Heaven for all the potheads, she had been planning on telling her aunt about finding Hitler. But now as she looked at her, with her glazed over eyes and blurry speech, she thought she should keep it to herself. Aunt Judy was doing well, kind of, and she didn't want to make it worse.

"I've been ok, I guess. I'm really bummed I can't get any more pot. I guess they must have found out about it and made it go away. The demon was still there though, and he gave it to me, but it just poofed out of my hands as I left the forest. I guess I could smoke it there, but who wants to smoke with a demon? Ugh, he's a nasty little fellow," Aunt Judy wrinkled her nose.

Kat wanted to defend the nasty little fellow, but she didn't want to tell her that she had been to see him. That could lead to a conversation about why there was no more weed in Heaven. That conversation would be about as pleasant as the one she had with her cat about his butthole. Which he was currently showing off to the other cats. They looked amused.

"Your cat has a butt!" Aunt Judy said, once again way too loud.

"I fed him, and it showed up. He is quite proud of it. No poop though, so that's good," Kat said.

"Well, now that is interesting," Aunt Judy said, not at all perturbed at Lucifer's butthole display. "I wish my cats could talk and eat."

The words were barely out of her mouth when all her cats started talking at once. Kat obtained a large bag of treats and handed them to her aunt whose eyes had gone wide. Aunt Judy took a large swig off the bottle of gin that was sitting on her coffee table. She took the bag of treats and shook them at her herd of felines. They ignored her. They were all babbling so fast, their words were unintelligible. Some of them were furiously studying their new parts, while the others were lifting their tails in order to show off to the other ones. A veritable cat butt festival.

Lucifer, taking advantage of the other cats' distraction walked up to Aunt Judy and asked politely if he could have one. As soon as he ate it, the other cats took notice and began to hoard around the now delighted Aunt Judy.

"Now everybody will get some, we need to take turns," she said seeming to regain some of her sobriety.

Her cats were not listening. They milled around stepping

all over each other, each asking to try one. Kat decided it was time to go. Aunt Judy might have lost her pot, but she would be occupied for a while. An eternity hopefully. Kat took solace in the fact that although she had been responsible for the loss of the weed, she had given something else to keep her busy.

"Hey, I think we're going to get going Aunt Judy. It was nice to see you," Kat said as she tried to locate her own cat in the mess of fur and cat buttholes. She saw he was already at the door and got up to meet him.

"Bye honey," Aunt Judy called as they left her to her hoard.

Kat lifted Lucifer into the basket, and they headed home. Now she was ready for a drink. And the first thing she did after parking her bike in her yard and stepping through her own door was to retrieve her bottle of bourbon from the kitchen. Not bothering with a glass, she took it to her sofa where Lucifer was waiting.

Kat had never felt rage like this when she had been alive. She had been plenty pissed, but this kind of anger came from some hidden spot deep down she hadn't had the courage to explore. It wasn't so much that she couldn't get high, it was more the fact that she had something that was all her own. Sure, she had her silly cat, but her pot was a symbol of her autonomy. Something that reminded her that even here, where every pleasure was just a thought away, the pot was something that ran out. She had to go and get it herself; it was her best reminder that she had once been alive. But not only had they taken it from her, but Aunt Judy too. Not to mention they had taken her ability to remove her damned halo.

She had her every whim on demand, but there was less joy in it. There was no effort involved. When she had put in a long night at work, grinding on laps and putting up with endless drunk dudes, counting her money was a rewarding experience. She loved the feeling of having earned her take. There were times when some guy whether generous or inebriated would simply hand her a couple of hundred just for standing there, it was great. But it didn't replace the feeling of accomplishment from the chase. Without the hunt, the kill was meaningless. It was like opening up a 1000-piece puzzle to find that it had already been put together.

That was what Heaven was like. All kill and no hunt. It was boring, soul crushing, and erased the individually and problem solving that feeds contentment. Heaven wasn't only a lie. It was unjust rewards. It sucked all the meaning out of existence. She thought she could understand why the angels were such assholes now. It gave them something to do, a goal. Devoid of opposition and challenge, their mission is to control and demean. They were the gatekeepers in Heaven, drawing satisfaction from displaying dominance and feigned superiority. She might understand why they were the way they were, but she would not excuse it.

"Kat...? Are you ok?" Lucifer asked her when she stood up and began to pace the room.

"I don't know man, I don't know," she said, honestly.

She was not ok with spending forever this way. She would not let herself be beaten into submission. Her father and aunt thought that they had everything they had wanted, but that wasn't enough. The material things that Heaven provided failed to provide the things that made one happy. She didn't have to look any farther than a bottle of scotch her father would never finish. Too afraid of Hell to see that he was already there.

"Come on Lucifer, we're going to find that bitch," she said.

"She's right next door," he replied with concern.

"Not that one, Lyla. I'm going to fucking kill her. Or mess her up real bad. Or maybe just talk some shit." Kat said.

"Uh ok then. Let's go," Lucifer said. "Um, Kat are you

sure that's a good idea?"

"No, but I can't think of anything else, we need to get out of here. So far, I haven't gotten anything but a stern talking to from Jesus," Kat said as she headed for the door. "You can stay here if you want. If I don't come back, go to Aunt Judy's, I'm sure she'll take care of you little buddy."

Lucifer looked thoughtfully, "No, I still want to come with you Kat."

"That's my boy, my ride or die. Let's do this," she said, and they walked out into the waning sunlight of Heaven.

She put him in the bike basket while Karen watched from her yard. Kat didn't bother acknowledging the middle finger she was throwing in her direction.

As Kat looked for Lyla, she realized she hadn't given much thought to how she would do the deed. Stab her. Shoot her. She needed something biblical, something old and barbaric. She wished now that she had bothered to read at least some part of the bible. She did remember something about a mob of dudes trying to rape an angel, but she didn't want any part of that.

How about a sword? She didn't know if there were any swords in the bible, but from what she did know, it seemed like the appropriate way to kill an angel. She imagined swinging it at her neck and lopping off the angel's head. Kat started to giggle. Lucifer turned his head to look at her with unease.

Kat peddled toward the angel bar and saw it was full of people. Lyla would surely be inside. She saw Jesus standing on the bar, he wasn't speaking, but she knew he would be soon. She stopped by a nearby tree still unnoticed by the angels, and leaned her bike against it. She helped Lucifer to the ground. A large heavy sword appeared in her hands. She started to walk toward the bar.

"You ready?" she asked her heavenly cat turned murder accomplice.

"I think so," he said.

She looked him over. His fluffy little face scrunched up in anticipation and his short little legs trembling. She wondered if he could get away fast enough. She had given him a voice and a butthole, what about wings? As the thought happened, two little wings sprouted out of his back.

"See if those work," she asked him. She hoped he could manage them better than she could.

Lucifer flapped his wings tentatively and his paws lifted off the ground, his eyes grew wide, and then he smiled his weird smile. A menacing little ball of fluff with sparkling wings. At the very least, they would make a scene. Again.

Lucifer chose to walk as they neared the bar. Kat spotted angel Lyla off to the side of the bar where Jesus was preparing to speak. She was talking to a delicious looking male angel with a head of blonde hair that hung to his shoulders. She did not notice Kat and Lucifer approaching them as her back was turned to them. The male angel's eyes grew wide as he saw them, Lyla turned to see what he was looking at. A hideous grin appeared on her face, and she looked like she was about to say something, but Kat didn't give her the chance.

Kat reached up and snagged the horrible angel's halo. She hefted the heavy sword and swung it at angel Lyla's neck as Lucifer lifted himself into the air. He floated and screeched at the two horrified angels as the sword cut through the air. Kat's aim was dead on, the sword connected with her neck and should have sliced clean through. But the second it hit her skin; it was no longer a sword. The bar erupted in laughter as Kat looked at the blue foam pool noodle she was now holding.

She brought it down and wished for a large knife instead. Lyla was standing still and silently gloating. Kat moved to stab her in the belly with her knife, but soon saw that what she now wielded was not a lethal weapon, but a large rubber pink dildo.

"You might want to hang on to that, Kat the whore," Angel Lyla said as the whole bar was laughing. But hey, at least she didn't call her Kathy.

Lucifer turned around in mid-flight and showed the whole bar his butt, the bar patrons gasped in unison. Kat dropped the dildo where it bounced and jiggled obscenely before becoming still, and turned to leave. Lucifer floated to the ground and followed her out into the night.

Kat didn't bother to retrieve her bike. She walked home with Lucifer by her side. She tried to hold her head up as she walked home in the dark, but it seemed too heavy. She felt so stupid, blinded by anger it hadn't even occurred to her that she couldn't even hurt an angel let alone kill her. *Stupid, stupid, stupid.* The stars shined with less intensity as she thought they had before. They seemed to be fading. The moon took on a milky appearance, as if it had grown a cataract. Tears stung Kat's eyes, and refused to retreat, even as she reached her home. She always hated to see her neighbors, but she was especially appreciative that they were hiding in their homes tonight.

As they walked through the door, Kat dropped onto the sofa, it didn't suck her in the way it had done. She just sort-of floated on the top of it, as if it was repulsed by her. And she could relate, as she was currently repulsed by herself. Lucifer walked over to hop up with her.

"Can I keep the wings?" He said.

"Sure, little dude," she said.

He snuggled up against her, folding his wings close to his round furry belly. She thought he might try and console her, but he stayed quiet. Kat had never been depressed. She had been plenty bummed before for various reasons, but nothing like she felt right now. The crushing sense of defeat and hopelessness were utterly foreign. She felt as if her whole being was being sucked into itself, as if she were a black hole. The despair she felt in Heaven was nothing she could have experienced when she was alive.

Kat had lived most of her life thinking that when she died, that would be it. Just nothing. An end of her being. She went through her ups and downs with a gratitude for her own life. She had been thankful for every day that she had because she had been certain that there was no life after death. It would simply be an end to consciousness. If she were lucky, she would have people who would remember her fondly. She hoped that she could do some good before she died and leave the world a little better than when she came into it.

Even without the promise of Heaven or threat of Hell, Kat tried to be a good person. She took a few liberties with the "good" part, but she had never hurt anyone. She did her best to help people where she could. She always returned the shopping cart to the corral and remembered to return her library books. She loved people, her cat, and she loved her life. She did her best to show her gratitude for being alive by not being an asshole. She made a lot of guys happy at least.

It took getting to Heaven for her to be a real asshole. Since she had gotten here, she had become hostile, mean, and now an attempted murderer. She didn't like who she was here. In fact, she hated who she was here. Her perfect body was a lie. The things she had enjoyed on earth held no meaning. She was lonely. She had been happy in life, but in Heaven, she was miserable.

Lucifer had begun to snore. She thought of what she had put this little creature through. All he wanted to do was make her happy. He had been created for only that purpose. She had drug him down with her. She thought of him screeching as she swung her sword. He was ready to watch her kill. Help her kill. She had corrupted this innocent little being who wanted nothing but to love her. And to show off his butt.

Kat peeled herself away from him and off the sofa, hoping he would stay asleep. His eyes stayed closed, and she tiptoed into her bathroom. She wished back her bottle of bourbon as she ran a bath. As she stepped into the tub and laid down, she took a large burning swig of the liquor. The warmth bloomed in her belly, a belly she wasn't sure she even had. Was this just another trick? A deception meant to make her think she really had a stomach. Just another filthy lie. She drank again.

She hadn't needed to shave her legs since death and so had no razor in her bathroom. She wished for one, and was surprised when one appeared on the side of the tub. An old-fashioned straight razor. She took another swig off her bottle and stared at it. She had thought she would just be nothing. Just a rotting corpse in a grave, without a brain, no consciousness. No pleasure or happiness, no pain or suffering, just nothing. She longed for that now. Just nothing. She took another drink.

Kat took one more drink, and thought that she had never been this drunk. Her thoughts were spinning, but there was no threat of puking. Just an endless cycle of dark despair. She picked up the razor, and without another thought, drew it upward from the inside of her left wrist to her elbow. The skin parted without any sensation at all. She repeated the action on her other arm. The blood poured out into the bathtub. She watched it tint the water pink. Her thoughts became slow and sluggish. Her vision grayed out and as she looked down at the water, she saw it was sparkling. Her blood was full of glitter. Because of course it was. She closed her eyes and her thoughts ceased.

"Kat…Kat, you're leaking," Lucifer said waking her up in the tub.

Chapter 21

Kat opened her eyes to a winged cat staring at her with his eyes full of worry. Lucifer licked her face, and her eyes filled with tears. She looked down to see that rather than a bath full of bubbles she was sitting in a tub filled with her own sparkling blood. Her arms were still open and her blood still leaking. As she looked at the open cuts still oozing, they closed, leaving no scars. She wasn't surprised but disappointed anyway. The one sure way to get to Hell was to kill yourself. Unless you were already dead.

"I'm sorry, dude. That wasn't cool," she said and scratched between his ears.

Lucifer kept his paws on the edge of the tub with his wings tucked against his body.

"Have you thought about talking to God?" he says.

"I haven't really. Not since I was a little kid. But I guess I did right before I died," she thought for a moment. "That does seem like a good idea, if he forgave my sins, it would stand to reason he would listen to me now. Maybe he'll let me leave if I just ask him? Ask and you shall receive right?"

"I don't see how it could hurt. The worst he could do would be to send you to Hell." Lucifer was wearing his strange cat smile and she grabbed his face between her hands and kissed the top of his head.

She got out of the tub, feeling no effects from the blood loss or the booze. She donned her Heaven robe and walked into her living room. She caught the pink donut box out of the corner of her eye and stepped into her kitchen for a donut and a cup of coffee to help her collect her thoughts before she left to meet God. Lucifer joined her at the table with his own bowl of food. She thought she would be repulsed by the smell. Instead, she was pleased at the sight of him enjoying it. Being dead sure changed one's perspective.

She wondered what she would say to God if she were allowed to meet him and then wondered if she would need an appointment. She decided she would just be honest. She would simply pour her heart out to him. If he were ultimately good, as she had been taught in church, he would understand. He would have compassion for her. He was God. The whole Hitler and Dahmer thing might just be something she didn't understand. He was her creator after all. And didn't she owe him the benefit of the doubt? Mysterious ways and all that.

After they finished the breakfast they didn't need, Lucifer and Kat stepped out into a brand new day. Kat was feeling optimistic and the birds and squirrels frolicking in the trees only fueled the feeling. She reached down to pick up Lucifer to put him in the bicycle basket, only to find him flying next to her.

"I would rather fly," he said, and she shrugged her shoulders in agreement.

She decided she would rather walk too. After her little incident with the straight razor, Heaven was beautiful once again. The sun was warm, but not too warm in the bright blue sky. She felt silly for not thinking of appealing to the big guy first thing. She had been dicking around with his underlings for too long. He loved her obviously; he let her in while St. Peter would have happily watched her burn. I mean if he could love Hitler, she should be easy.

Jeffery was leering at her from his ugly little yard, but her mood was such that even he couldn't bring her down. She smiled at him and in return, he gave her a look of perplexed disdain before they started down the road. Lucifer flew next to her as she walked. She enjoyed her walk but felt an apprehension as she reached the doors to Heaven's Administration building. She paused with her hand on the door, wondering if she was doing the right thing. She looked at Lucifer who appeared to be having no such trepidation, he was happily flying next to her. Any god that would create such a creature must be good. She pulled open the door and walked in.

The large foyer was dim in comparison to the bright sunlight of the day. The deep gold tones of the décor seemed heavy and constricting despite the cavernous size of the room. Other than Chad at the front desk, the room was empty. She could feel his disapproving eyes on her as she walked up the red rug to his desk. Lucifer landed and walked with her, folding his wings to his sides and adopting a reverent look.

"I'd like to speak with God please," Kat said, mimicking the expression of her cat.

Chad lifted a perfect eyebrow, "Oh really, and why do you think he would want to talk to you?" he said.

She was about to reply when a low rumbling shook the building and a booming voice said, "Come child," the voice of God said. The hallway to the left began to glow.

Chad looked terrified as he waved his hand toward the hallway to God. She nodded her head in thanks. Kat and Lucifer left Chad standing there with his hand extended as they moved toward the lighted hallway. It was much the same as the one that led to Jesus, except there were no other doors. There was only one large golden door at the end of an unnecessarily long hallway. Candles provided the light as she moved toward the door. Once again, she was rethinking her decision, but it was much too late to turn back. God had summoned her, and she doubted she could turn around now anyway.

The door swung open before she had a chance to open it. Light assaulted her as it poured from the room, and she stood there stunned and afraid to enter. Lucifer let out a little whine and huddled against her legs. She bent to pick him up. Her eyes did not adjust in the way they would to sudden sunlight. The light instead faded until she could make out the shapes inside the doorway. When she was able to step past the threshold, she found that it was not a room. She was standing on the clouds as she had waiting to reach the gates of Heaven. There were no walls, just blue sky and clouds. God sat waiting on an elaborate throne in the expanse of the endless space.

"Hello, my child, do not be afraid," the deity said.

Fat chance, she was terrified. Although of what exactly, she wasn't sure. She stopped and bowed her head as she neared him. He appeared as she had thought he would, an old man with a head full of gray hair and a beard to match. His robe closely resembled hers.

"I didn't expect you to look like what I imagined," she said.

"I appear to each differently, but always as the way each expects me to," he said. "I understand you are unhappy here."

"Uh…" she stammered, wondering if she was going to blow it. "I don't think this is the place for me. What I mean is, thanks for the salvation and creation and all but I think maybe I should be in the other place." Kat said. Lucifer tucked himself down in her arms. He was hiding his face from the lord.

"Your discontent concerns me, but would you choose

eternal suffering over my holy light?" he said.

"Why is there suffering at all, you could make it so there is not. But instead, you chose to set up this weird game where you allow horrible things to happen to make people prove they love you. You damn people to Hell for not believing in you while you refuse to provide any real evidence of your existence. It's kinda fucked up," the angry and rambling words just sort of fell out of her mouth. Lucifer was shivering now.

"Do you dare to judge me? To question my divine authority? To love and worship me is my greatest command. All must suffer to know my grace. The suffering is a test of my love. To love the one who hurts you is the greatest test, and all must pass to receive my grace in Heaven," God said, his irritation was apparent. "You have been forgiven for your sins, but I understand you want to leave Heaven. You will not be allowed to leave Heaven. You have proved your love when you chose to repent to spare your soul from Hell. Your soul is mine for all of eternity."

Kat knew exactly what to say to God. She was not struck with a blank mind as she had been with the angels. She wanted to say that only a narcissistic dickwad would create such evil in order to satisfy his own ego. Only a truly horrible and malignant being would enjoy watching their creations suffer and then demand love to avoid more suffering and pain. Only a sadistic sociopath would revel in the power to create fear and pain and call it love. She did not say any of this though, Lucifer was shaking in her arms, and she did not think that this god would punish her for her insults. She had no doubt that He would punish this helpless little cat instead. He would know that it would hurt her more to see him suffer than any pain he could inflict on her. She had spent most of her life thinking that God was a just a myth, now that she had met him she knew that she was wrong. God does exist, but he is an insufferable dickwad.

Kat turned and walked away, afraid that as she got to the doorway, he would not let her leave. As her foot crossed into the hall, a cold blast of air hit her from behind. She waited until her entire body had made it into the hallway before she turned to look. The door closed, and the candles in the hallway had been extinguished. God had spoken all that he had to say to her. She knew she could never, or would never worship such a rotten being.

Lucifer didn't raise his head until he felt the sun on his fur. "It's ok buddy. Fuck that guy. I think we'll go talk to Amon. He must have some idea of how to escape. God, like Heaven, is nothing more than a powerful illusion. He is not great, he is not all powerful and he is not just or kind," she said.

She walked home with her cat in her arms. When she got home, Jeffery was still in his yard. He looked at her with his creepy smile. She ignored him and walked inside.

"I thought God was supposed to be good," Lucifer said. "I don't understand."

Kat understood his confusion and his subsequent disillusion. She had asked many questions as a kid about God and his mysterious ways. Why did kids get cancer? Why would God answer some prayers but not others? Why was there so much pain? "God works in mysterious ways," was the answer. She decided that that meant that either He did all that stuff on purpose, or just didn't have control over it, or that He just didn't exist. She didn't want to believe He was just a dick, so she chose to believe He wasn't real. Even as she thought her last living thoughts, she hadn't believed He was real. Her dying brain spurted out prayers that were simply a reflex due to the dogma she had been taught as a kid. She hadn't really believed then, but her sincerity was irrelevant. All that mattered was that she was saying what His fragile ego wanted to hear.

"He's just a bully who is way too full of himself. We don't need Him. He is just desperate for us to think so. Here, how about a treat? You have been very brave," she said, and he shook his head no. It pained her to see him upset. She picked him up and kissed his head.

Kat sat down with him on the sofa. Lucifer relaxed and settled into her lap. She looked at him as he closed his eyes and imagined what he might have looked like as a kitten, although he had never been one as far as she knew.

She missed Buster, and wondered how he was doing in Hell. She realized she was no longer afraid of Hell. She wasn't afraid of God either. Her thoughts turned to Amon and the portal to Hell. He had told her that the fruit rotted when he tried to bring it down. He also said that when he came up, he took his demon form. The portal transformed things, but did that mean that they couldn't survive the trip? But did that even matter? She didn't think so, he had been alarmed when he tried and then stopped. He had no desire to come into Heaven, in fact he was afraid of it. Maybe the fear or lack of it was the key.

The fruit only existed in Heaven, so maybe it was unable to exist in Hell. But the demon didn't die when he moved through, only changed. Did the portal only destroy things that were not living while transforming the things that were? These were questions that could be answered, and might just be her ticket out of Heaven. Science bitches.

Lucifer had fallen asleep and although she wanted to jump up and run to the forest to test her theory, she didn't want to disturb her cat.

Chapter 22

Had she been alive, her lap would have been numb if she had allowed her hefty feline to sleep this long on her. She was beginning to become anxious as she waited for Lucifer to wake. She looked down at his peaceful little face one more time, before lifting him up off of her and placing him on the sofa cushion.

"Hey," he said, annoyed like a real cat.

"Sorry, I have to go talk to Amon. I have a few experiments I want to try with the portal. I think we might be able to use it to get out of here. I will need his help," Kat said. Lucifer just nodded in agreement.

They set out once again, this time the sun hung a little lower in the sky. Kat thought about taking her bike, but she wouldn't be able to get it through the thick trees. If she left it resting where she entered the forest, it could give away her secret. She chose to walk, and Lucifer chose to walk with her. She still found it a little jarring to see him flying anyway. She still hadn't found the heart to tell him how silly he looked with his wings.

When she first met him, Lucifer was more like a toy. A moving stuffed animal, but as she continued to give him more freedom to choose, he had changed. He wasn't the same obedient thing with his only directive to please her, and he had come to discover his own likes and dislikes. He had developed his own personality and desires. He was still thoughtful and devoted to her, but he was becoming his own cat. Did all the creatures manufactured in Heaven have the ability to develop their own will if given the chance? Were Aunt Judy's cats now starting to assert their own will? If so, Aunt Judy would have her hands full.

But what about the squirrels and the birds and other creatures? Were they just puppets of sorts that helped create the ambience of Heaven? She thought of the blood smeared on Jeffery's face and the horrible smile underneath the gore. Did he have human versions of these creatures to play with? She shuddered. That blood came from somewhere, did his divine victims feel that pain as his human ones did?

Kat shivered, no longer wanting to entertain those questions, but finding herself unable to stop. Why would God allow such behavior when He could simply stop the killer from having the urge? She thought she knew the answer, but it was almost too horrible to articulate even in her thoughts. God either knew or couldn't stop it, or He just didn't care. She wanted to think it was the former, but after meeting Him, she suspected it was the latter. His ultimate objective was His own glory and worship, the sin and bad deeds just didn't concern Him. She had often wondered why a loving god would create such a place as Hell. It was one of the reasons she stopped believing in the first place. She thought now He did it to make sure His creations had to make the choice to love Him, in spite of all the fucked-up things He did to them.

But could it also be that He didn't have the power He portrayed Himself to have? She hadn't known a lot of narcissists, but she had encountered a few. The ones she did know weren't just liars, but frauds. They built a façade of strength and caring to hide the fact that they were but empty shells who needed constant attention in order to continue to fool themselves and others that they were indeed who they pretended to be. Did God let really let people suffer in order to prove their love, or was that just part of the show? Would people choose to love Him if they knew that He only had the power to punish or reward them after death, but not to control life on earth? Did God even create Heaven or Hell, or did He simply install Himself in a position to appear that He did. Kat was starting to think that His whole shtick was just a game. Maybe He wasn't all-powerful at all; maybe His only power was to fool some that He was. The ones who weren't fooled were sent to a place called Hell.

"We're here," Lucifer said, pulling Kat out of her thoughts, much to her relief.

Kat stepped into the dense copse of trees, and noticed the sound of the waterfall had diminished from the last time she was here. She hoped that wasn't a sign that Amon had gone away with the pot. The thought brought anxiety and rather than calmly make her way through, she started to frantically push and pull at the tangled branches. Succeeding in making the whole thing more tedious. Meanwhile, Lucifer with his small but fat little body had no trouble at all.

"What's taking you so long? You good?" He called from the other side.

She paused, regrouped, and began to make her way more carefully. She almost materialized a machete to cut through them, but was glad she didn't. That might bring attention as the bike had. She was already concerned that Heaven had somehow found out and started to make it go away. She broke through to the other side, and saw that the rainbow looked as if it had been painted with watercolors. The waterfall nothing more than a trickle.

Staring at the once magnificent waterfall, she could not only see the change but feel it as well. Something was wrong. She went to the space in the hole and tossed down a pebble. Lucifer was right by her side. He didn't seem as frightened as before. After a time, Amon's fuzzy face appeared, but different. He had a more human quality than he had before. It did nothing to improve his looks.

"Hey, what's up?" Amon said.

"You tell me. Shit seems weird over here. One of the angels found out about the pot and made it disappear. I can't get it out of the forest. Aunt Judy's too," Kat said.

"Hey, want to see something?" Lucifer said to the demon, and began to turn his back end toward him.

"Not now dude," Kat said, in a firm but gentle tone.

"All the cats in Hell do that, you're learning," Amon said to the winged cat and winked in the most disturbing manner. Lucifer beamed his weird smile at him. "I think the portal is breaking down. Are you still trying to get to Hell?"

"I am. I met God, and He won't let me go. I want to try to go through the portal," she said.

"Well, you should probably hurry, but like I told you things don't come out the same way. But that might be different now that the portal is crumbling," he said.

"You look more human, maybe Heaven isn't effecting you so much anymore. Can you try bringing a piece of fruit through again?" Kat said.

"Sure," Amon said, and no smoke at all came from his mouth. His teeth appeared to be duller too.

Kat stood up from her kneeling position and trotted to the nearest fruit tree. While her back was turned, she heard Lucifer say to Amon, "You sure?"

"He's sure dude, give it a rest," Kat called not bothering to confirm that Lucifer was once again trying to display his butt to the uninterested demon.

She picked two pieces of fruit, one to go through the portal and one for Amon to eat. Sensing she was running out of time, she hurried back and handed the two pieces of fruit to Amon. He left one on the rocks.

"I'll be right back," he said and disappeared. He returned only a moment later. "It made it, but it was all bruised and squishy. Not totally rotten as the last time. He picked up the other piece and took a large bite. He grimaced.

"This tastes different. Too sweet," he took another bite to confirm his findings. "Yup, not terrible, but not great either." He tossed the half-eaten fruit to the ground. "Now what?"

"I think we should try something living," Kat said, and looked around for a squirrel or something before she remembered there weren't any in this space. She looked at Lucifer, and then said to Amon, "Would you try to come up here? The portal isn't having the same effect as before. Maybe it won't be so bad?" She gave him a sheepish smile.

"I really want to help you out, but I don't know. I only tried it once, and it sucked. Could your little friend get through? If he can, I'm sure you can too," Amon said, saying what Kat had been thinking.

"I'll do it," Lucifer said.

"No dude, you might get really hurt or die or something," Kat said.

"I want to, I don't want you to stay here, and I don't want to be here without you. Aunt Judy is cool, but she has too many cats. If I can't be with you, I don't want to be," Lucifer said.

Before she could stop him, Lucifer opened his wings, half jumped, and half flew into the space where the demon sat. Amon brought his arms up to catch him and avoid a face full of cat. Amon didn't give her any chance to protest, and they were both gone down into the depths of the hole to Hell.

Kat paced for what seemed like an eternity, and for all she really knew it could have been. She put her ear to the hole, hoping to hear something. She heard only silence. She didn't know what to do. She prepared herself to go in after them, but as she stepped forward and hunched down, she was confronted with the face of the demon. Their foreheads butted together.

"Ow, you got to be more patient, Kat," Amon said rubbing his head, which was still terrifying. But less furry than it was when he left the last time. She noticed he was alone.

"Where's Lucifer?" She asked, afraid of the answer.

"Why in Hell of course," he replied smiling. "They both are in fact. The little furry one is the one you are asking about I assume?"

"Yeah, what happened?" Kat asked.

"He freaked out a bit. That's what took me so long. His wings are gone, and he can't talk anymore, but he is ok. Maybe a little banged up. I took him to my house and tried to calm him down. I don't have any cat food, but I gave him some milk and he seemed to chill. You should come be with him. As far as I can tell, he lost his heavenly traits. But is otherwise ok. I think you'll be alright, but the trip is rough."

Kat was about to jump down the hole, but as she moved closer, she thought about her aunt and her father. Did she really want to leave them here? She didn't.

"I have to go get my aunt and my dad. I don't know if I can get them to come with me, but I have to try," she stood up and turned to leave.

"I don't know how much longer this place is going to be here, and I don't know of another portal. This one wasn't supposed to exist at all. Just a weird glitch. You sure you don't just want to come now?" Amon said.

"Yeah, I have to try. I'll hurry," she said. "Do I need you to get through?"

"I'm not sure, but I'll stay close. Hey hurry, I don't

want to babysit your cat," Amon yelled to her as she made her way back through the dense trees.

Chapter 23

K at was closer to her father, so she decided to head there first. She hadn't wanted to visit him again after the last time. Seeing him in a perpetual state of drunkenness was a burden she didn't want to bear. She thought he might be easier to convince than her Aunt Judy as well. She didn't think she had much time, and couldn't quite shake the feeling that she might be squandering it. Both her aunt and her father had been afraid of Hell, convincing them to go there now would be near impossible, but she had to try.

Kat wanted a bike now, and one much like the one she had left at her home appeared. She hopped on it and began to peddle as fast as she could. The wind blew her hair back as she rode over the bumpy road.

The landscape blurred by as she rode. When she got to her father's home, she dumped the bike and stumbled over her feet as she hurried to get to his door. She knocked much too hard on his door and her foot did an anxious tap dance as she waited for him to answer. When he did, she could tell he was hammered. More than hammered.

"Hey dad," she said. "Could you get sober for a minute? I need to talk to you."

He looked perplexed, hurt maybe, but the glazed over look left his eyes, "I'm ok, what's wrong?"

Kat didn't really know how to explain it to him. She had been so focused on getting here, that she hadn't thought at all about what to say. If she said the wrong thing, he would dismiss her and be stuck in Heaven. It was kind of a lot of pressure, and now she found herself speechless. But she had to say something. Time was running out.

"Dad, I'm going to Hell," she wasn't good at this. "What I mean is, my neighbor's a serial killer. People here suck, I met a demon, and he said that Hell is way better." She was blowing this, and yet she couldn't seem to stop herself from fucking it all up. Her dad was staring at her with clear but confused eyes. She had to keep trying. "I saw Hitler, Dad. Hitler is here, God is an asshole. I found a way out. You can bring your dog. I already sent my cat."

"Wait now. I don't understand what you are saying. You met a demon? Don't you think he might be lying to you?" He said, and she couldn't help reflecting on how much she missed having a dad.

"I thought about that," she considered telling him about Aunt Judy and the weed, but the dad thing stopped her. "Look, I met God and Jesus, Heaven is a lie dad. They want you to stay drunk or otherwise immersed in the façade, but it's all fake. God is just a self-absorbed asshat. Please will you come with me? I'm going to try to get Aunt Judy to come with us too. When I get there, I might be able to contact mom too. God told me he needs her to suffer. See? That's super fucked up. Please dad you have to trust me." She was rambling now, and was unable to tell if she had gotten through to him.

"I don't know. You really shouldn't trust a demon honey. Are you sure?" He said, and she could tell it wasn't going to work. How do you go about convincing someone to change the things they had believed their whole lives? She didn't want to leave, but she was starting to become concerned the portal may collapse and disappear. Tears filled her eyes as she thought of leaving him here.

"Please dad, come with me. The portal is going to close soon, and I don't know if there will be another chance." Kat gave it one more try, but was getting ready to leave.

"Well, ok. Let me get my dog," he said, and Kat was sure she had misheard him.

"What? Really?" She said.

"Yeah, fuck it. I'm tired of being drunk. I always thought God was a bit of a dick anyway. Could Hell really be that bad? I mean if Hitler is here," he said.

Kat threw her arms around her dad, "Come on, get your dog, we have to hurry."

Her dad whistled and, Beelzebub came trotting up. She motioned to her bike, and she wished one for her dad too. They got on and began to ride, Beelzebub ran beside them. Her aunt's house wasn't very far, and her fear that they might miss their chance was becoming unbearable. She hoped that with her dad here that Aunt Judy would be easier to convince. But Aunt Judy had been more religious and fearful of Hell. Kat didn't think she would come along. Then again, she had been wrong about her father.

When they got to Aunt Judy's, Kat was in a near panic. She was almost sure they wouldn't make it. Her and her father dumped their bikes, and pounded on the door. Aunt Judy answered much quicker than her father had, but was in the same inebriated state. Her eyes had the milky sheen of a long drunk. She did not look happy to see either of them, her cats either. She answered the door but was one of her cats that answered first.

"Go away. She doesn't want to talk to anyone," a large tabby said. An orange one, who sat next to her, stared at them with malicious intent. "We're all she needs."

Aunt Judy nodded in agreement and said, "Yeah, I'm good. I've got all I can handle right now. Unless you got some pot that is…" Her words slopped out of her mouth.

"Aunt Judy," Kat started to say, but found as she had with her dad that she didn't know how to continue, her dad stepped in.

"Judy, we're going to leave this place. It's not cool. Kat found a way out. You can take your cats…?" He said, but reluctance filled his voice as he looked at the number of cats mulling around her. "Hey, can you sober up just a bit so we can talk?"

"Yeah, fuck you. I don't want to leave here; can't you see how happy I am?" The words sprayed out of her mouth like spittle, and she slammed the door.

Kat could hear one of the cats complain that they didn't get to show anyone their butthole through the closed door. Her dad was about to knock again, but she stopped him.

"Dad, we have to go. Maybe when we get there, we can find a way to get her," Kat said as she turned to leave. He just nodded and followed her.

Beelzebub struggled to keep up as they rode toward the trees that concealed the portal. His tongue dangled from his mouth as he galloped along with them. When they reached the trees, he paused, sniffed, and began to whine. Kat and her dad dropped their bikes.

"Come on, it's right through here," Kat said. "Dad?"

She had turned her back to her dad as she started to push through the trees, but when she didn't hear him follow, she turned to look behind her. Beelzebub was running down the road, her dad was not her dad. Lyla stood in his place, wearing a self-satisfied smile.

"Planning a trip?" she said.

"What the fuck? Where is my dad?" Kat said.

"He's where he should be, drunk in his house. He didn't even notice when I answered the door. His stupid dog didn't notice I wasn't him either. Followed us out the door like a good boy."

Kat didn't want to waste any more time, but she couldn't seem to help herself from asking, "How did you do that? I couldn't change my face when I tried, not even with the halo."

"I'm in good with God, I tell him every day how great he is, Jesus too, the secret to Heaven is good old fashioned ass kissing. Gets old, but is totally worth it. Play the game and you get to do whatever you want. You should've seen the look on your face. Whore."

Kat was livid. For the last damn time, she was a slut not a whore. Now she wondered if it was really her Aunt Judy she was talking to. She feared she had no time left now. If she had any hope of getting out, this was her chance. If she fucked around with this angel, she could miss it forever.

Kat plunged into the thick trees. Trying not to panic this time, but couldn't help it. Now that her secret was out, she figured a machete wouldn't hurt. One appeared in her hands, and she began to chop and slash at the foliage. She was frantic, the closer she got the more convinced she was that she had missed it. When she made it through, she saw that Lyla had followed her, easily walking through the path she had made.

The trees had all turned the color of raw sewage and oozed a terrible liquid that reminded Kat of the time she had left a bag of lettuce to rot in her fridge. A brown foul-smelling mess was all that remained of the green trees that had been here. The waterfall was dried up and the grass surrounding it was melting along with the trees. The stones looked to be intact, but they had a faded quality, as if they were growing soft.

"Ugh, this place is gross. I'm glad it will be gone soon.

You too, whore. Heaven will be a better place without you. I was sorry this place took so long to disintegrate, but now I'm kind of glad it didn't go with the weed. I had wanted you to get stuck here, but making your afterlife miserable has grown stale."

Kat had never wanted to punch someone in the face so badly until now. Rather than give in to her urge, she made for the space in the stones, the entrance to the portal to Hell. She bent down ready to dive in, not wanting to wait for Amon to come help her though. It was time to get the fuck out of Heaven.

Lyla wasn't done with her though, and she followed her there, giggling and sneering, staying close behind her.

"Go Kathy, the whore, run away little whore. Kathy, Kathy, Kath…" Angel Lyla's voice cut off as Kat turned and grabbed her by the front of her robe. She yanked her into the hole along with her.

"Come on bitch, we'll finish this in Hell," she said and it was her turn to giggle as the angel screamed.

Chapter 24

The ride was rough, as Amon had promised. Heaven was, as Kat had imagined, Hell not so much. She landed hard with a fistful of Lyla's robe in her hand. She had her eyes closed as they went through the portal, and they flew open as she landed with a thud on a patch of compacted sand. What she noticed first was that she had narrowly missed a rocky outcrop of rocks, what she noticed second, was that Lyla was no longer the blond-haired supermodel beauty she had been in Heaven. Her hair was still blond, and she still retained a semblance of her angelic self, but that was where the similarities ended. Kat thought it was unlikely that anyone would ever suspect she had ever been an angel.

Lyla, still in her robe. Which in Heaven hung loose and flowing over a slim figure, now fit snug and tight, and looked to Kat to be terribly uncomfortable. Her once flawless complexion was now an alien landscape of pits and valleys with rising angry red pimples that looked as if they had been lurking under the surface and had finally seized their moment to break free. She was sitting with her legs crossed in a daze, and Kat thought she might be hurt. Kat herself felt a little beat up, as if she had been in a car wreck. Which she didn't find too surprising, as she had in fact, been in a car wreck. But all things considered, she felt ok. The former angel on the other hand did not look any kind of ok.

"You alright?" Kat asked, and it was hard not to feel sorry for her the way she looked now.

"I don't know." And she began to cry, big deep sobs that wracked her whole body. Fat tears ran down her bumpy cheeks and snot began to trickle out of her nose.

"Hey man, I'm sorry," Kat wasn't sure yet if she was sorry, but it seemed the right thing to say. She put an arm over the once beautiful former angel.

Lyla put her head down and sobbed harder. Kat continued to pat her gently on the back, while she waited for her to get her shit together. Kat thought it might be a while, so she took her own assessment. The arm that had been broken was healed. But there was a scar where the bone had poked through. There was a dull ache in her back, and she felt like she had to pee, which was now an unfamiliar sensation. But a strangely welcome one. Her hair felt like a matted mess, and she saw blood on her knee where her robe had torn. Pain. Not unbearable, and not totally unwelcome. Kat poked her finger into the wound, winced, and smiled.

Beyond the sand where they sat, were the rocks they had almost landed on, and a vast lake. Kat noticed that not only was it not made of fire, but it did not smell like sulfur either. It wasn't crystal blue as the pond in Heaven, but dark turquoise. She couldn't see to the other side of it, but noticed a few sailboats floating out in the middle. The sky in Hell was blue, but a tad darker. Birds and clouds dotted the sky. As she looked up, she realized how cartoonish the sky had been in Heaven and wondered how she could have thought it was so pretty. The sky here wasn't a perfectly painted work of art, but a beautifully imperfect reflection of something she might have seen on earth. As Kat looked up, she almost felt at peace.

Almost…because Lyla was still losing her shit. Kat put both arms around her, hoping to calm her. She regretted pulling her down, regardless of whether she thought the awful angel had deserved it. Kat wished she wasn't such a pussy, but she just couldn't bear to watch Lyla this way.

"Hey, it's going to be ok. Calm down, we'll figure this out," Kat said. "Let's see if we can find someone to help."

Lyla looked up at her with swollen eyes and sniffed a wad of snot back up into her nose. "I'm sorry," was all she said.

Kat helped her to her feet, not an easy thing to do. Together they walked along the beach. She looked around to see where they had exited the portal, but she couldn't find it. At the edge of the beach and surrounded by rocks, Kat saw a set of stone steps leading up from the beach. With her arm still around her shoulders, Kat led Lyla towards them. The sand was soft, but coarse under her bare feet and she was hoping to find some shoes soon.

As they reached the bottom of the steps, a man came bounding down them.

"Hey, why didn't you let me know you were coming?" The man said.

"Amon?" Kat replied.

"Yup, you ok? Who's this?" He said.

Kat was a little slow to reply, as she was staring at the demon. He had told her he looked different in Heaven, but he hadn't mentioned how handsome he was. Kat was struck dumb at the sight of him. A lock of chestnut hair hung over his forehead, and she couldn't stop staring at his eyes. She tore her gaze away. Suddenly afraid she was staring like Chad the admin angel. She wasn't trying to creep the guy out. In fact, she was hoping to get to know him better. Much better, a warmth spread between her legs.

"This is the angel I was telling you about," Kat said.

"The one who tattled about the weed?" He said, and Lyla looked away.

"Yeah, but she's had a rough ride. Go easy on her," Kat said, she had just gotten her to stop crying and didn't want her to start again.

Amon held out his hand and took Lyla's hand to help her up the stairs. Together, Amon and Kat helped the former angel climb each step. Lyla wasn't used to her new size, or pain, or the rest of it. Kat realized it might have been a long time since she had felt such things. Rather than hate the angel who had given her so much grief in Heaven, she found she pitied her. She had been head mean girl in charge in Heaven, in Hell she was a pathetic nobody.

The trip up the long stone staircase was tedious as the two pulled Lyla along. Each step was a laborious feat. Even with the help, Lyla was panting and sucking wind by the time they reached the top. A large stone monument stood at the beginning of the stairs.

It read:

1. Do not give opinions or advice unless you are asked.

2. Do not tell your troubles to others unless you are sure they want to hear them.

3. When in another's lair, show him respect or else do not go there.

4. Do not make sexual advances unless you are given the mating signal.

5. Do not take that which does not belong to you unless it is a burden to the other person, and he cries out to be relieved.

6. Do not complain about anything to which you need not subject yourself.

7. Do not harm little children.

8. When walking in open territory, bother no one.

Kat watched Lyla's eyes move over the words, her face emotionless.

"These are the eight rules of Hell. Follow these and you will be in peace," Amon said. "There are a few other things you should know as well. Your bodies are like they were on earth, except you will not grow any older than the age you were when you died. You will eat and sleep as you did. You can be injured, but you will heal with time. You will be provided with the basics, a home, food and other necessities but will need to earn luxuries. I'll take you to my house first, so you can get your cat and then we'll get you set up in your own place."

"What about her?" Kat asked.

"We can stop by the Hell intake office and drop her off on the way," he replied, and Lyla began to wail. *Fuck, she just stopped.*

"She can hang with me until she gets settled," Kat said, and put her arms around the bawling former angel.

"Suit yourself, you don't have to though. She will be in good hands as long as she obeys the rules," Amon said, amid Lyla's fresh cries.

"I brought her here, I need to see that she is taken care of," Kat said.

Lyla's whining ebbed a little, as they began to walk to Amon's place. He led them down a concrete road, which was hard on her feet. Lyla waddled behind them. Trees and grass flanked them on either side, not all the grass was green, some of it had weeds and brown spots. She saw houses similar to the ones in Heaven, but these were not perfect. People were in their yards, tending to gardens or weeding flowerbeds. She saw people painting and mending fences.

She saw fat people, skinny people, older people and young ones. Some were attractive, and some not so much, but all of them seemed content. They waved as they walked by, and Amon and Kat waved back. Lyla kept her head down and her hands to her sides. Amon stopped in front of a pleasant-looking little house, with a neat yard. A sprinkler rained water over a lawn which when she looked closely, she saw had a few little patches of crab grass. *How utterly wonderful.* In the window, a furry black and white cat poked his head through the curtains. Lucifer began pawing at the pane when he saw them approach.

"This little fucker has been waiting for you," Amon said as he walked them up to his front door.

"I bet. Will you be able to help me find my other cat Buster? I'm pretty sure he died in the crash with me," she said.

"Shouldn't be too hard to find. Satan makes sure to reunite those who want to find each other in the afterlife. He gets a bad rap, but he's a pretty decent dude," Amon said as he unlocked his door. He noticed Kat watching as he turned his key. "Most people respect each other's space here, but not everyone. Better to be proactive about these things."

Lucifer bounded out the door as soon as it was open. He bounced at Kat's feet, and she picked him up. He snuggled under her chin, and she kissed the top of his head.

"Hey, little dude." Kat said over his purrs.

She carried him inside Amon's humble little house. As she walked in, the strong odor of the litter box assaulted her nose. *Well, I guess poop is a thing in Hell.*

"Uh, sorry about that," Kat said to Amon.

Amon just shrugged and motioned for Lyla to sit down. She had stopped crying but was still sniffling. Kat took a seat as well, still holding Lucifer, who made it obvious that he was not ready to be put down. Amon went into the kitchen where she heard the tinkling of glasses and the sound of running water. He returned with and handed one each to her and Lyla. Kat drank greedily, and was pleased to find that the water quenched her thirst.

Amon took a seat across from them in a large overstuffed green chair. He reached into a side table and pulled out a pipe and bag of weed. He packed the bowl and offered it to Lyla first, and when she refused, handed it over to Kat who did not.

"Thank you," she said as she lifted it to her lips and lit it. She drew in a deep lungful of smoke and then let it out in a series of hacking coughs. When she could speak again, she said, "Oh yeah, I'm going to like this place."

Lyla began to cry again.

Chapter 25

Kat set Lucifer aside on the sofa, he protested a little and she thought he might take to Lyla's lap. But instead, he laid down and glared up at her, Lyla did not seem to notice. Kat was beginning to get concerned that the trip to Hell might have scrambled her brain a bit. She had yet to say anything other than she was sorry, Kat bet she was. And yet she still felt responsible for her rash decision to grab her and pull her into the portal. She had wanted to punch her in the face, but now she felt bad about it.

"Ok, where's the cat box?" she asked, and Amon pointed down the hall. Kat followed his direction and found the little bathroom where he had placed the litter box. She picked it up and took it outside, found a bush and dumped the whole thing. Buster had been trained to go outside, and she was hoping she could do the same with Lucifer. When she returned, Amon was still sitting in his green chair.

"So, I guess we should go to the office you were talking about, and find our permanent homes? I really would like to find Buster and see if I might be able to talk to my mom. I doubt she'll listen, but I think I should tell her about God and what a dick he is. At least she should know I'm not burning in an endless lake of fire." She said to the now good-looking demon.

"Sure, it's not far," he said and looked down to her feet. "They'll have some shoes and other stuff for you too. I'd like to see you out of that robe." He said with a wink. Kat thought she was going to faint.

Kat, Lyla, and Lucifer walked out the door with Amon. He led them down a narrow road lined with more houses. They passed a small park, which had several wooden tables. At one of the tables sat a couple of people scowling at each other over a chess game. She was afraid the whole thing might get ugly, until one of them blurted out "Checkmate!" And they both began to laugh. She smiled and waved as she walked by. Kat had almost forgotten what good-natured laughter sounded like. All the laughter she heard in Heaven was at her own expense. She cast a sideways glance at Lyla.

On the other side of the park, there was a large brick building. The sign on the front of the building read "Hell Intake Office". Three short steps led up to the front door. Amon stepped in front of them to open the door for the two ladies and the cat. Lyla entered first.

The lobby reminded Kat of the last DMV office she had been too. Cool, clinical, with polished cement floors, and florescent lighting. There were several service counters, but only one was occupied. A gray-haired lady with silver horn rimmed glasses was looking down at a piece of paper with a stern look. She was holding a pen up to her lips and was nibbling lightly on the cap. She looked up at them as the door opened.

"Can I help you?" she said, not cold, but not warm either.

"These two just arrived from Heaven," Amon said as they approached the counter.

"Heaven? Amon, have you been poking your head

into Heaven?" The lady said. Amon answered her with a smile.

"Ok ladies, let's get you set up. Let me check my notes," the lady said as she peered over the top of her glasses. She put aside what Kat saw was a crossword puzzle and pulled a large binder from somewhere under the counter. She dropped it on the counter and began to rifle through it, until she seemed to find what she was looking for.

"Let's start with you, um, Kathryn?" The lady said.

"I'm Kathryn, but you can call me Kat," she said.

"You can call me Gertrude, Kat. Nice to meet you. It says here you were allowed entrance into Heaven. I've never met anyone who came to Hell willingly. I assume you went through the portal?" Gertrude said.

"Yes, ma'am. My mom is still alive and is worried about me. I've been able to see her but not contact her," Kat said. "I also wanted to find my cat, Buster. He died with me."

Gertrude looked down at Lucifer, "Not this one, I guess. Good thing you croaked young. You might have ended up an old maid drinking wine out of a box with 20 of those things," Gertrude let out a hoarse cackle. "Ok let me assign you a home and I'll have someone bring your other cat. This one came from Heaven. I must say that is a new one for me too. As far as your mom goes. Come back here after you've cleaned up and gotten settled. We don't like to grant those kinds of requests. Proof of the afterlife gums up the works, but exceptions can be made. I'll see if I can arrange a brief meeting. Probably end up in some goofy ghost show." She looked at Lucifer who was presenting his butthole to the new lady, which she ignored. She scribbled something on a piece of paper and handed it over the counter to Kat. "Ok now this one, Lyla is it?"

"Yes," Lyla sniveled. "I don't belong here. Can I go back to Heaven?"

"Uh, Lyla it says here you were a real bitch. You

definitely belong in Heaven," Gertrude cackled again. "You're going to have to take that up with the big guy my dear. Looking at your file, I don't think he'll want you here. But it looks like you were the one that had the portal destroyed so I'm not sure what we can do for you now. You might just be shit out of luck." She handed Lyla her own slip of paper. "Here are your quarters for now. You'll be fine as long as you follow the rules."

Lyla began to bawl yet again. Kat thought about having her come stay at her place, but as she looked at the sniveling former angel, she decided she would rather not.

"I'll come check on you in a while and see how you're doing," Kat said, feeling like a jerk, but she just couldn't handle anymore whining. Lyla dropped her head, took her little piece of paper and walked out of the building to find her rightful place in Hell.

"Ugh, I really wish you had left her there, Kat," Gertrude said.

"Sorry about that, it was kind of a reflex. I feel bad about it though. Even if she was a real bitch," Kat said.

"Meh, shit happens. Well go find your place. It won't be like Heaven, but you will be able to make it better the longer you're here. We've stocked it with some essentials. Come back and we'll see what we can do about your mom." Gertrude said this time with a warm smile.

"Ok, thanks," Kat said.

Amon walked her and Lucifer to the door and they stepped out into the daylight. Kat noticed it was darker than before and saw that there were gray clouds in the sky. She smelled the damp scent of rain. Amon reached for the paper Gertrude had given her and she let him have it.

"This isn't far from my place. I'll take you there. I bet Buster will already be there," he said.

Kat was pleased, and she found it hard to believe she

had been afraid of him. She realized that she had not looked at herself since getting to Hell. *Jesus Christ, I probably look like hell,* she thought, and a small laugh escaped her lips. Amon gave her a puzzled look.

"I must look awful," she said.

"You don't look like you did in Heaven, but you're alright. I wouldn't throw you out of bed," he said and winked.

Kat remembered rule number 5 and thought that he had just given her the mating signal. She blushed. They walked on and soon came to a small brown house. It was plain and the yard was all dirt. It was clean though. A small mat sat in front of the door and Amon bent down to lift it up, revealing a key. He picked it up and slid it into the lock, but didn't turn it. He stepped aside and let Kat turn it and open the door to her new home.

A lamp burned on a table beside a humble tan sofa. Sitting in the light was a very irritated-looking cat. Buster. Kat ran and picked him up, and cradled him in her arms. She began to cry. He stiffened at first, but finally gave in and snuggled up under her chin. Lucifer stood in the doorway with the same irritated look that Buster had just had.

She put Buster down and invited Amon to come in. He sat on her little sofa and prepared a bowl to smoke. Buster and Lucifer eyed each other suspiciously. They walked over to each other, and Buster hissed and swiped at the interloper. Lucifer hunkered down and closed his eyes. Buster sniffed his head before turning and returning to his place on the sofa.

She walked into her kitchen and found it stocked with if not her favorite foods, stuff she could eat. And she was hungry. She grabbed an apple out of a bowl on the little table, which sat under a small window. She took a bite, and found it to be just a little mealy. Not great, but not terrible. There was an alarming lack of donuts. The bright little kitchen was done in a pale yellow, with cream-colored curtains over the window. Also, not great, but not terrible either. She was sensing a pattern here.

She continued to munch her apple and made her way down a short hallway to her bathroom. She looked in the mirror and the apple fell out of her hand and into the little sink. Her hair was a mess. Her freckles were back, and she saw a tiny red blotch of a budding pimple on her chin. A hairbrush sat on the counter along with a toothbrush, toothpaste, and a few other toiletries. She looked at the toilet in the corner next to the shower, and remembered she had to pee. She shut the door and sat down. She could hardly believe the relief she felt. She got up and flushed. Before leaving, she ran the brush through her hair, and took another look. She was far from perfect, but she liked herself better this way.

She checked out her bedroom and closet. The furniture could have come straight out of a motel 6. She had a small closet where she found a few items to wear. They didn't look new, but they were clean. *Good enough,* she thought as she pulled on a fresh pair of jeans to replace the dirty and torn robe she was wearing. She found a fresh shirt which just so happened to have a Slayer logo on it and no fucking glitter. She walked back out to find Amon waiting for her.

"Well, what do you think?" He asked. He was sitting between the two cats who seemed to have settled down now that they couldn't see each other.

"Not bad, better than Heaven, no donuts though," she said and he handed her the pipe.

"There are donuts in Hell. They're all the old-fashioned kind, but they're pretty good," Amon said.

They smoked a while and made some small talk. Her head filled with smoke, she found she couldn't stop staring at Amon. She noticed his gorgeous eyes crawling all over her boobs.

"Hey, do you want to see my bedroom?" She asked

him.

"Sure," he replied.

As they walked into her room and shut the door, she could hear Lucifer and Buster growling at each other. *They'll work it out,* she thought as she pulled her t-shirt over her head.

Chapter 26

Kat forgot all about Lyla, her mom, her awful time in Heaven, and her two cats for a while. Mediocrity seemed to be the theme in Hell. That was her first impression at least. Amon changed all that. Sweaty, panting, and quivering all over, Kat untangled herself from her demon lover and collapsed on her bed.

"Wow," Amon said. "We should do that again sometime."

"Damn straight," Kat replied, still trying to catch her breath.

The light outside the window in her bedroom had darkened, but it wasn't quite night yet. A loud crash of thunder shook her little place and a bright flash lit up her room as she heard the sound of pounding rain on her rooftop. She got up and went to the window. A dark red downpour obscured most of the landscape and left a blotchy red film on the glass.

"Is that blood?" She asked Amon.

"Yeah, Satan is a Slayer fan. It happens from time to time. Seems to be good for the grass, but a bitch to get out of your clothes. Do you mind if I hang out until it passes? It won't be too long, I don't want to overstay my welcome," he said.

Kat thought she might be in love.

"Sure. I think I need a shower. But I need to get back to the intake office and see about my mom. I still have to figure out what I'm going to tell her. I don't want to freak her out," Kat said as she made her way to the bathroom.

"Mind if I join you?" Amon said.

"Why the hell not?" Kat laughed.

They squeezed together in the shower. The water wasn't much more than a trickle, and she thought she might not get much cleaner than when she went in, but once again, the demon brought her to ecstasy. She booted him out when it was done, so she could wash her hair and clean up. She got out and toweled off. Noticing that the towels weren't quite as fluffy and soft as they were in Heaven. All of Hell gave her that impression. But the relief of not having to contend with the bullying angels, serial killers, and the weird rantings of a demigod made it all worth it.

Amon was lying in the mess they had made on her bed when she came out of the bathroom. His smile was infectious, and she couldn't help but beam one back at him. Before she dressed, she inspected herself in the mirror. Freckles, moles and the scars of her life had all returned. She was no longer the strange, perfected version of herself. The Heaven filter had been removed. Gone was the sense that she was looking at a cartoon version of herself. It had never been perfect hair or unblemished skin that had made her beautiful, instead it was the scars and imperfections. Receipts from a life well lived.

She dressed in what she suspected were Hell's version of thrift store clothing, but that too was a small concession to the indignity of the perfection of Heaven. The jeans she pulled on were soft and broken in, and the t-shirt had thin spots in the fabric, signs that it had been well worn. Her clothes had seen some things. Her hair was still wet, and she found that when she tried to apply the makeup in her bathroom, she had to remember how to do it. She opted to wear just a little, and to let her hair dry in its natural state.

When she walked into her living room, she found both her Heaven and Hellcat sitting on opposite sides of the lumpy sofa. At least they weren't fighting. She set some food out in separate dishes for them, and they hopped off the sofa eating side by side. Buster doing his best to pretend like the other wasn't there.

She couldn't hear the rain on the roof anymore and Amon was getting ready to leave.

"You should be able to get back to the office on your own. Hell has a great comedy show if you'd like to check it out some time," he said. "A bunch of great bands too."

"That sounds great, how do I reach you?" Kat replied.

"I left my number by your phone. See you later," he said as he opened the door and walked out into the blood-soaked street.

"Bye Amon," she called, realizing that she hadn't struggled to remember his name.

She made sure her cats were still ignoring each other, and left a few minutes after Amon. When she stepped out of her door, she saw her neighbor in his yard. Once again, she was struck with a sense of familiarity. The guy had on a black turtleneck and slacks. He had a kind face, and his brown hair was cut in a way that resembled a helmet. He was examining the blood spatter left from the storm. He was so caught up in his study that he hadn't noticed her watching him.

She watched for several minutes before he looked up and waved at her.

"Hello, I'm Carl, Carl Sagan," he said. "You must be new. This rainfall was fascinating. So many things to learn about this place."

Well, how the fuck do you like that? "Nice to meet you,

I'm Kat." She said.

She walked out of her humble yard, stepping in a puddle of blood. Her shoes squished as she walked down the road. She didn't mind. The sun was setting, and she could hardly take her eyes off the bloody sunset. Blue and purple bathed a sky dotted with the evaporating dark clouds. The sun itself was a deep orange ball of fire. She was so enamored with the view that she almost didn't notice the office building as she approached.

She walked up the short steps and opened the door. Inside Gertrude was chewing on her pen and glaring at the crossword puzzle. She looked up when Kat walked in.

"Damned puzzles. I get to the end but have yet to finish one all the way. It's been hundreds of years now, and I've never completed one. I got them all when I was alive. It's Hell though what do you do?" She said. "You are here about your mom I presume? It's well past closing time and I've been waiting for you to return."

"I am. Thank you. I have been able to see her, but I haven't been able to connect. She is grieving and I just want her to know that I'm ok. Not sure I can explain all that has happened since I died, but I think if I can let her know I'm not burning, it will help ease her mind. She is a devout Catholic and is terrified about Hell," Kat said.

"I was afraid of Hell once, until I heard about Heaven. That place sucks. I can arrange a brief meeting with her. I will caution you about telling her too much about the afterlife, strong beliefs can be hard to overcome. You could make it worse if you tell her too much," Gertrude said, her tone stern but caring.

"That's what I was thinking. There really is so much I want to say, but the most important thing she needs to know is that I'm not suffering. Every time I've looked in on her, she is crying. I can't be at peace until I can help her," Kat said.

"Ok, well, it isn't easy, and it will hurt. A lot. You will feel drained and will probably need to rest for a while after. I will arrange to have someone take you home," Gertrude said. "Do you see that door over there?"

Kat looked in the direction that Gertrude pointed in, and saw a glowing. Either it had not been there before, or she hadn't noticed it.

"I do," Kat replied.

"When you open it, you will be transported to where your mom is. She will see you as you are now, but in spirit form. You will have around five seconds, and you will not be able to touch her. So, speak clearly and quickly. This will likely be your only chance. You ready?" Gertrude peered over her glasses at Kat.

"I think so," she said as she walked to the door.

She was afraid it would be hot to the touch because it was glowing bright red. She felt an immense urgency, but also hesitation. Finding the right words in the right moment was not her thing. If there was one thing she fucked up consistently, it was this. She tried to collect her thoughts, but they were scrambling around her brain like cockroaches caught in a sudden flick of the switch. It was now or never though, and her hesitancy was only prolonging her mother's pain. She closed her eyes and put her hand on the doorknob, turned it, and pulled it open.

She was in her mother's bedroom. The space was in disarray. Her mother was a neat and tidy person, and Kat thought for a moment that there had been some mistake. Clothes were strewn carelessly about the room and a thin layer of dust coated almost every surface. *How long had she been dead?* She might have turned and gone back if she hadn't seen her mother lying on the unmade bed. She wasn't crying this time, but she was staring glassy eyed at the ceiling. For a horrible split second, she thought her mother might be dead, but then she stirred. Kat moved toward the bed and noticed that her feet were floating inches off the floor. Her mother had not noticed her yet.

"Mom?" She said.

Her mother turned her eyes to her. She blinked, and then sat up.

"Kathryn?" Her voice barely a whisper.

"I'm ok mom. I love you. I'm not hurting. I'm at peace," She said. *Holy shit, I didn't say anything stupid.*

Her mother reached for her as she was wrenched back through the door. It happened so quickly that Kat didn't have time to react. She was thrust back into the office building in Hell and unceremoniously dumped on the floor. The glowing door was gone, and she just laid there on the floor. She felt as if her whole body had been drained of not just blood but all her energy too. She didn't think she could move. The place where her back had broken ached and throbbed and she had to check to make sure her arm bone was still inside her skin. She hadn't been in this much pain since lying on the side of the road thinking about feeling up the paramedic.

Obscuring her pain and fatigue was an overwhelming sense of relief. A skeptical person might see a ghost and think they were dreaming or hallucinating. If there was any advantage to her mother's religiosity it was that Kat knew that her mother believed that she had been in the room with her. She would not doubt that she had just seen her daughter from beyond the grave. That knowledge brought comfort to Kat, and she knew that her mom would be able to go forward without the fear that her daughter was burning in Hell.

There was the lingering fear that when her mother did make it to Heaven, and Kat had no doubt that she would, that she would discover its rotten secrets. That God had no interest in whether someone had been a good person, He didn't care about the suffering of humans, and His only motivation was the selfish indulgence of His own ego. Her mother had the unshakeable conviction that God was great, and she hoped for her own sake that when she did get to Heaven that illusion would persist. That she could be fooled for eternity and not have to witness the countless evil people allowed to populate paradise because they were willing to praise a deeply flawed deity.

Kat opened her eyes, disoriented and unable to determine just how long she had been lying on the floor. She wasn't sure if she could move, but she heard footsteps coming toward her. A face appeared above her. A handsome face she couldn't help but notice. He kneeled down and slipped his hand under her head. She barely noticed as he lifted her head up and brought a cup to her lips. He tipped it up and she parted her lips to drink. A burning sensation flooded her tongue, and she closed her eyes. She let the liquid creep down her throat.

"Here you go. A little vodka goes a long way," he said. "My name is Lars, and I'm going to help you get home. You're going to be weak for a while. I'll be right back."

He set her head back on the floor, and she heard him walk away. When he returned, she turned her head to watch him approach. He was short and built thick, with light brown hair and matching goatee. He was pushing a wheelchair. He parked it next to her and bent back down to lift her up. She was still in a lot of pain, but some of her strength had returned. She was able to sit up and he hefted her mostly limp body into the chair. She couldn't help but be a little embarrassed.

He wheeled her out the door into the darkness of her first night in Hell. Most of the bloody rain had soaked into the ground and the smell of iron had started to dissipate. The moon was purple she noticed. She didn't know if it were filtered by clouds giving it that hue, or if Satan simply liked that color. She thought she might ask her neighbor. If he didn't already know, he would be trying to find out. Kat smiled. There was science in Hell.

Lars pushed her past what seemed to be a bar where raucous laughter bled out through the doors. People congregated outside talking and laughing. Some of them had horns, and she wondered what she might look like with a pair. She rolled over a bump, and it reminded her that her spine had been severed at some point, and she cried out.

"Sorry," Lars said. "We're almost there."

He wheeled her up to her door and when the knob turned easily, she realized that she had neglected to lock it. Inside, her cats waited for her on the sofa, and they both jumped down to greet her. She reached down and tried to pet them both at the same time as they pushed each other out of the way.

Lars left the chair outside her door and helped her stand up. He walked her inside and to her bedroom. Firm but gentle, he laid her down on the bed she hadn't made. He removed her shirt and jeans and pulled the blanket up to her chin. Kat would have found the gesture erotic, if she had not been in so much pain. Instead, she took comfort in the compassion of the act. Lucifer and Buster jumped up and lay on either side of her, trading dirty cat looks over her hips. She thought she heard a low growl out of Buster.

"I'll be right back," Lars said as he left the room.

She heard the clinking of dishes and the beep of a microwave, and soon he returned with a bowl. She could see steam rising from its contents. As he brought it closer, she caught the scent of chicken soup. He brought it to her and helped spoon into her mouth. It was thin and tasted weak, but warm and soothing. When she had finished, he set it down on the table next to her and removed one of the pillows propping her up.

"Get some sleep and you'll feel better in the

morning," he said.

Kat was struck by the concern and caring in his eyes. And she was reminded of the stunning lack of empathy of those in Heaven.

"Thank you. Are you some kind of nurse?" She asked, but her eyes were growing heavy, and her words were mushy.

"I was a fireman in my life, and I still like to help people. They call on me when I am needed here. It was a brave and selfless thing you did tonight. I'm going to leave my number, give me a call if you need anything," he said.

Kat nodded her head and smiled at him as he left the room and her home. She thought he looked like an angel. *Hmm, a Hell's angel* was the last thing she thought as she drifted into a dreamless sleep.

Chapter 27

Cat awoke to not one, but two cats sitting on her chest. Buster was staring at her and the look on his face was an abject threat. *Feed me or die and I will eat you,* he seemed to say. Lucifer's face told her he thought Buster was capable of following through. She took each one's furry face in turn and kissed the tops of their heads. The pain in her back and arm was present but much less intense than it had been before. She swept the two unearthly felines to the side and sat up.

The sunlight that filtered in through her window cast a pink glow about the room. The bloody rain of the night before had left a sticky film, and she realized that she would need to wash her windows. She would have other chores as well, but rather than dread them, she found she was looking forward to them.

She stretched, blinked and wished for a cup of coffee. When a fresh steaming perfect cup did not appear, she threw off her covers and set her feet on the floor. A low throb of pain coming from her back made her cautious when she tried to stand. When she was sure she could walk, she made her way to the kitchen. Buster walked directly in front of her feet in a deliberate attempt to trip her, while Lucifer walked directly behind at a respectful distance.

She went to the coffee pot sitting on her hideous yellow countertop, and searched for some coffee. She found it, her second favorite brand. She started it and attended to her cats. One waiting patiently while the other gave her the death stare.

"Come on buddy, I came all the way to Hell to find you. You can't be mad forever," she said to Buster who meowed at her in response indicating that he could indeed be mad forever.

She filled the two dishes and watched as they both ate as if they had been on the brink of starvation, instead of only being a matter of hours since they had last eaten. As she watched them eat, she poured herself a cup of coffee. She took a sip of the black brew. It was hot, bitter, slightly acrid, and totally wonderful. She sweetened it with a touch of sugar and a splash of milk. In her pantry, she found a package of powdered donuts. A cloud of sugar puffed around her face as she took her first bite. She took a sip of coffee to wash it down.

She walked around her house, wearing just the pair of panties she had slept in. She thought of Lars, and how he undressed her. In spite of her nudity, he had simply tucked her in without the slightest hint of creepiness. She made a mental list of the things she needed to do. Wash the windows, wash her sheets, and so on. She finished her coffee and started a load of laundry. All the little mundane things she never had to do in Heaven, she found that there was a certain satisfaction in these tasks that she had missed.

She pulled on some clothes and walked the outside perimeter of her new home. She found some cleaning solution and rags under her kitchen sink, and she washed the blood off of her windows. She had a little tree in her yard, which appeared to bear some kind of fruit. She got closer and saw little apples growing on it. A squirrel eyed her suspiciously from one of the branches and chirped a warning.

She had a pathetic patch of grass that looked to have the potential of being a decent lawn if she put in a little effort. A wayward dandelion sprouted from the middle of it, she thought about pulling the weed, but decided to leave it. It was her only flower, and she decided she was fond of it. She was terrible at gardening and had a brown thumb, but figured she had all of eternity to learn. She was looking forward to the challenge.

Excited about her new existence and all the possibilities, she went back inside. A knock on the door came as she was making her bed. Hoping it was Amon, she was more smitten with him than she would have liked to admit, she rushed to open it. Her stomach dropped when she opened the door and saw what was standing on her porch. Terror struck her mute.

She stared unblinking at the monster at her door. She had to crane her neck upwards to see his head. If Amon had been scary, this dude was like her every worst nightmare come to life. His red skin stretched over the sharp features of his face. Two large curling goat horns protruded from his bald head, his eyes were bulging black orbs, which reflected her own face frozen in a mask of pure fear. Under his pointy nose, his lips stretched into a wide smile revealing razor teeth. When he spoke, Kat shuddered.

"Please allow me to introduce myself," the horrible monster said. "I'm a man of wealth and taste." He smiled the most hideous smile and laughed a laugh that loosened her bowels. "That never gets old! Hello Kat. Do not be afraid, easier said than done I understand, but I promise I will not hurt you. I have been waiting to meet you," the creature said in a soft voice that contradicted his horrifying appearance. He held out one huge hand, "I'm Satan, please may I come in?" He said.

The world went gray, and she was sure she was going to faint. She fought hard to hang on to her consciousness and was able stay upright although her knees turned to rubber. In a reflexive action of habit, she took his hand, and he began to shake it gently. His hand was soft to the touch, and the surprise of its texture helped to calm her. But she still found herself unable to speak.

"Come on, I'm not that ugly," Satan said despite being that ugly.

Kat stepped back and allowed the creature to enter. Lucifer leaped off the sofa and raced into her bedroom. Buster opened his eyes for only a moment before closing them again and going back to sleep. Satan took a seat next to him and petted his head. Buster opened his eyes and began to purr. Kat frowned and took a seat next to the large red guy, trying to keep from being pulled into the hole his huge ass created.

Satan pulled a pipe out of the pocket of the black velour jumpsuit he was wearing and offered it to Kat. Thinking it was a bad idea to refuse Satan, she put it to her lips keeping her eyes on the monster. He produced a small flame from the tip of his finger and touched it to the bowl, which was filled with fragrant green buds. She drew in deeply.

"I'm sorry I scared you. I don't usually show up like this, but I just had to meet you. I consider you a bit of a hero. You're the first soul since myself to escape from Heaven. You are very special Kat," Satan told her.

She handed him the pipe as she exhaled. The softness of his voice in contrast to his looks were jarring, but she felt herself starting to relax.

"That's very kind, uh Sir," she said.

"Call me Satan," he said, his words choked off as he exhaled them in a huge cloud of smoke. "This is from my special stash." He winked and she hoped he wasn't flirting.

"Ok Satan. I really appreciate you allowing me to contact my mom," she said. "God and his angels weren't what I expected. You either I guess."

"No problem. The least I could do. I hate needless suffering. God really is an asshole. Pompous piece of shit He is," Satan's eyes narrowed and Kat recoiled. "He is great at fooling people, but He's nothing but a fraud. His angels are dicks too. I see you brought one of them with you," he scowled, and she thought she was going to faint once again.

"Sorry about that. I didn't really mean to. I panicked when the portal was breaking down. I just grabbed her without thinking," Kat said.

Satan took another hit off the pipe and passed it to Kat. The springs in the sofa creaked as he sunk lower into it. Kat was becoming accustomed to him, and starting to like him as well. Not as much as Amon, but Satan, like the demon had an honesty about him that made it hard to be afraid of him. At least once you got past his terrifying looks.

"Meh shit happens. Hell isn't perfect and not everything here is wonderful, but it's fair, just, and honest. Most of my time is spent righting His wrongs and thwarting His cruelty. And yet I'm the one who gets treated like the asshole," Satan said with despair. "That's why I'm so glad you're here Kat. You've done more to expose His unchecked narcissism than I have in thousands of years. After you get settled, I hope you are willing to help me in my mission. That is to save people from the perversion of Heaven. It's one hell of a task," he snickered at his own pun. "But I think you might be the one to help me do it. I can't offer you much. I don't have the same power as God, but I think you will find satisfaction in the job."

Stoned, Kat tried to process the fact that Satan had just offered her a job.

"Well, sure. Heaven really was awful. My neighbor was

Jeffrey Dahmer. My mother will be horrified," she said.

"Jeffrey Dahmer?" Satan asked.

"A serial killer who killed and ate his victims. Really gruesome. I think he is still doing it in Heaven," Kat replied.

"Wow, what the fuck?" Satan said. "Well, hey Kat it's been real. I will catch up with you later. Think about what I said. I think you and I together can be a real force for good. Explore Hell for a while and we'll talk again."

Satan got up but left a canyon in the shape of his enormous butt in her sofa. He gave her an apologetic look. "Sorry, I'll get you another. Perhaps you should come to my place next time?" He said, "See you later."

He gave Buster one last pat on the head and walked out her door, ducking his head to avoid knocking his horns against the frame.

Lucifer poked his head into the living room, and she patted the spot next to her on the couch. He jumped up and sat next to her. She petted him and he snuggled against her as Buster glared at them from the other side of the dented sofa. So far, she has fucked a demon, appeared to her mom as a ghost, and become friends with Satan. It was a lot to take in. Not to mention the bloody rain and the angel she had dragged to Hell.

Hell seemed to have much more potential and now she was anxious to see what it was all about. Satan's weed had alleviated most of her pain and she thought she would give Amon a call. Maybe he could show her around. She reached over to the phone and the piece of paper he had written his number on. Next to the number, he had scribbled a tiny pentagram. Cute. She picked up the phone, took a deep breath, and dialed.

She had to pull the phone away from her ear when the grating sound of a fax machine transmission pierced her ear. She was about to hang up thinking she had misdialed when she heard the demon pick up on the other end.

"Hello?" Amon said.

"Hey, it's Kat. I was hoping you might show me around Hell," she asked hopefully.

"I'd love to. I know a decent restaurant and we can see a show. I'll come pick you up in a few hours." He replied.

"That would be great!" She said. She had meant to play it cool, and she sounded anything but.

She hung up the phone and bounced into her bedroom. She flung open her closet only to find the perfect outfit was not there. She pawed through her meager wardrobe and finally settled on a little black dress that fit not quite right, and a pair of slightly scuffed black stilettos. She checked herself in her mirror. Not perfect, but it would do.

In her bathroom, she spent some time on her makeup and found a curling iron that only sparked a little when she turned it on. She looked at the clock and saw that she still had an hour. She sat on her Satan's ass-damaged couch and waited.

She was starting to drift off when she heard the rumble of an engine outside. A soft knock came at her door, and she got up much too fast to answer it. Amon stood at the door holding a bunch of almost wilted roses. Kat's heart leapt to her throat, and she blushed.

"Hello, you look stunning," said the demon. He didn't look so bad himself in a pair of jeans and studded leather jacket. His bare chest glistened under his jacket, and Kat couldn't help but stare.

"Thanks," she said. "Let me put these in some water."

Forgetting that she should invite him in, she darted to her kitchen where she filled a chipped water glass and dunked in the sad looking roses. She doubted they would last long, but she took a long sniff and they smelled heavenly.

Amon waited at the door, she hooked her arm through his, and he walked her out to his waiting motorcycle, a mean looking Harley. She hiked up her dress and mounted the seat behind him. Her dress rode up to the middle of her waist and her almost bare ass sat on the seat. The engine started and the vibrations promised a pleasant ride.

He pulled up in front of an Italian restaurant where they had a mediocre dinner of pasta and stale garlic bread. Amon gave her the rundown of how Hell worked, and she hung on his every word. After, he took her to the cliff where she arrived where they watched the sun go down. As it dipped below the horizon, he turned to kiss her. Which turned into touching, which turned into fucking.

"The show starts in a few minutes, you ready?" He asked her as they pulled on their clothes.

Kat dizzy with contentment, said, "I am."

They mounted his bike and rode to the bar she had passed the night before. They waded through the crowd at the entrance and found a couple of seats with a good view of the stage. He ordered a couple of whiskeys, and they arrived as the lights dimmed. The crowd began to cheer, as a tall skinny man walked out behind the curtain and into the spotlight.

"Thank you, nice to see you on this wonderful night in Hell," George Carlin said.

Oh yeah, I'm going to like this place.

END

About the Author

Erin Louis is a former adult entertainer with three non-fiction books about her life as a stripper as well as several short fiction stories.

She has a lifelong love of horror and dark humor.

Please check out her website at https://www.erinlouis.com/

OTHER HELLBOUND BOOKS

Stripper Noir

"I'm pretty much out of my "detective phase" now that I've finished Random, but I wanted to check it out. It's a nice detective murder thing with a twist and a very nice look at Vegas and the strip club scene. It's very accurate (as far as I know) strip club description and you never see that in a book, so that was nice. And a nice view of Vegas one doesn't usually get. I really enjoyed it." - Penn Jillette

Exotic Dancers are dying at an alarming rate in Las Vegas.

Former LVPD detective, Frank Michi, is roped into helping not only his former partner, but also the New Jersey mobsters who run the strip club, to unmask the psychopath who is running amok killing the dancers.

Can he figure it out in time - before more girls are brutally murdered?

The Toilet Zone: Number Two
"Restroom reading at its most terrifying!"

Imagine, if you will, you're traveling through the unknown, hellbound, with no roadmap or stars to guide you. The light fades as you descend into a shadow realm where supernatural terrors make their lair and evil lurks at every turn. Here, dead things don't always stay dead, for this is a world where things that shouldn't be… *are*, and things that should be are not.

In this world, it takes between 2,500 and 4,000 reading words to pay a visit to the smallest, but terrifyingly necessary, room, and stories are written precisely to chill the bones as you wait for nature to make its call.

You open up the book, and one of the 32 tales skulking within its hellish pages chooses you…

It's too late to turn back now. You are about to set foot into another dimension, so best watch out for that signpost up ahead…You've just crossed over into... The Toilet Zone

The Erotic Odyssey of Colton Forshay!

Colton Forshay dreams himself into a bizarre sexual dystopia - a world in which nothing is as it should be, it alternately rains semen and menstrual blood, sickening sex acts and sexual violence are the norm, and the currency is deviant sexual acts. In this dream world, Colton inexplicably finds he has gotten his dog pregnant and his wife is brutally murdered as a contestant on a popular TV show.

At first disturbed, then intrigued - and shamefully aroused - by his dreams of the other world, Colton is drawn in deeper and begins to spend more time there with the help of sleeping pills. His real-world wife forces Colton to see a psychiatrist, who encourages him to explore the dream world. And thus, our hcro embarks on an odyssey with his dog/son, Eric, to discover the disturbing truth behind his dream world.

This is fantastical tale populated by a whole host of bizarre characters, set in an incredibly peculiar world. Chock-full of startling, sexy imagery and told with incredibly dark humor, Colton Forshay is a bizarro tale both engaging and disturbing.

The Horror Writer
"The most definitive guide into the trials and tribulations of being a horror writer since Stephen King's 'On Writing.'"

We have assembled some of the very best in the business from whom you can learn so much about the craft of horror writing: Bram Stoker Award© winners, bestselling authors, a President of the Horror Writers' Association, and myriad contemporary horror authors of distinction.

The Horror Writer covers how to connect with your market and carve out a sustainable niche in the independent horror genre, how to tackle the writer's ever-lurking nemesis of productivity, writing good horror stories with powerful, effective scenes, realistic, flowing dialogue and relatable characters without resorting to clichéd jump scares and well-worn gimmicks. Also covered is the delicate subject of handling rejection with good grace, and how to use those inevitable "not quite the right fit for us at this time" letters as an opportunity to hone your craft.

Plus... perceptive interviews to provide an intimate peek into the psyche of the horror author and the challenges they work through to bring their nefarious ideas to the page.

And, as if that – and so much more – was not enough, we have for your delectation Ramsey Campbell's beautifully insightful analysis of the tales of HP Lovecraft.

Featuring:

Ramsey Campbell, John Palisano, Chad Lutzke, Lisa Morton, Kenneth W. Cain, Kevin J. Kennedy, Monique Snyman, Scott Nicholson, Lucy A. Snyder, Richard Thomas, Gene O'Neill, Jess Landry, Luke Walker, Stephanie M. Wytovich, Marie O'Regan, Armand Rosamilia, Kevin Lucia, Ben Eads, Kelli Owen, Jasper Bark, and Bret McCormick.

And interviews with:

Steve Rasnic Tem, Stephen Graham Jones, David Owain Hughes, Tim Waggoner, and Mort Castle.

**A HellBound Books LLC
Publication**

www.hellboundbooks.com